Ghosts of Savannah

Terrance Zepke

Pineapple Press, Inc.
Sarasota, Florida

Inquiries should be addressed to:

Pineapple Press, Inc.
P.O. Box 3889
Sarasota, Florida 34230

www.pineapplepress.com

Library of Congress Cataloging-in-Publication Data

Zepke, Terrance
 Ghosts of Savannah / Terrance Zepke.
    p. cm.
 Includes index.
 ISBN 978-1-56164-530-5 (pbk. : alk. paper)
 1. Ghosts--Georgia--Savannah. 2. Haunted places--Georgia--Savannah. I. Title.
 BF1472.U6Z459 2012
 133.109758'724--dc23
                          2012014580

First Edition

Design by Jennifer Borresen

Contents

Introduction

Savannah is one of the prettiest towns in America. But don't take my word for it. It was actually on Forbes' America's Prettiest Towns list in 2010. It has also received numerous other awards, such as "20 Sweet Spots for Summer Travel (MSNBC.com), "Best Southern City" (*Southern Living*), "50 Best Romantic Getaways" (*Travel & Leisure*), "50 Great Cities to Visit in America" (*London Daily Telegraph*), "Top U.S. Tours" (TripAdvisor), "Ten Best Walking Cities" (*Walking*) "Top Ten Cities in the USA" (*Conde Nast Traveler*), and "Top 100 Places to Retire" (*Money*).

I've never heard anything negative about Savannah from tourists, except about the heat and humidity during summer. It is, after all, the heart of the Lowcountry. Even the surrounding rivers and estuaries do little to cool the city during the peak of summer. Yet everyone, from history buffs to "foodies," falls in love with this charming city.

I think the layout of the city attributes to its likeability. In the historic district, all the buildings and houses are part of public squares and parks that also contain shady trees and either stately monuments or picturesque fountains. This is due to the vision of the city founder, General James Oglethorpe. He established the port city in 1733 and began building these squares.

He built six: Johnson Square, Wright Square, Ellis Square, Telfair Square, Oglethorpe Square, and Reynolds Square. The remaining eighteen squares were added later: Franklin Square, Warren Square, Washington Square, Liberty Square, Columbia Square, Greene Square, Elbert Square, Orleans Square, Chippewa Square, Crawford Square, Pulaski Square, Madison Square, Lafayette Square, Troup Square, Chatham Square, Monterey Square, Calhoun Square and Whitefield Square. Today, there are twenty-two squares. Elbert and Liberty Squares were lost to "progress": a government building and roadway. These squares add up to 2.2 square miles. This is the largest National Historic Landmark District in America.

The only problem I can find with Savannah is that there is so much to see and do that it can be overwhelming. I'm one of those tourists who like to see and do everything with the thought in mind that I may never get back, so I need to "do it all." In a town like Savannah, this is a tall order. I have visited on numerous occasions and still haven't done it all!

The city is best known for its rich history and architecture, fine food—and ghosts. With more than a thousand historical buildings and homes, there is plenty of architectural diversity, ranging from Greek Revival to Regency. This makes it the perfect backdrop for the well-known Savannah College of Art and Design (SCAD). The campus includes sixty buildings and one of the most impressive galleries in the city. It seems as if every other building in sunny Savannah is either a yummy restaurant or notable historic attraction.

Be sure to read the About Savannah and Visitor

Information sections of this book for more about the many ways to experience Savannah. Everything from creepy hearse tours to scenic carriage rides are offered from early a.m. until the wee hours of the next a.m. And don't forget that there are over 200 festivals (including the awesome Savannah Book Festival) held here every year.

But this is a ghost book and that is what the focus is on. And rightly so! There are so many ghosts that they must surely bump into one another! See the Haunted History section of this book for a comprehensive discussion of this pretty city's sinister past that helps explain why it is one of the most haunted cities in America.

No matter how you choose to explore Savannah, you must allow time to sample its fine cuisine. Remember that Savannah is home to Lowcountry cuisine and the legendary Chef Paula Deen. She owns a popular restaurant and you'll see her cookbooks and food products sold in many shops throughout the city. With so many options, it is hard for even the toughest critic to find fault. For example, one restaurant features locally caught shrimp served every way imaginable. And the best part is the restaurant is haunted so you may have a ghostly encounter while you're there! Read "Shrimp Factory" in this book for more about that particular ghost.

While you'll learn a great deal about the city of Savannah after reading this book, its emphasis is on ghost stories of Savannah. You'll find out why an exorcism had to be conducted at the Hampton-Lillibridge House, about the ghost cat at the Davenport House, the rowdy ghosts at Pirate's House who can be heard demanding more to drink, and the female spirit of the Kehoe House. You'll be surprised who haunts the Old Candler Hospital and why. You'll learn what is arguably the most haunted place in Savannah—and much more.

If you're into ghosts and planning an overnight visit, you may want to consider staying in one of the city's haunted inns or B&Bs—if you're brave enough. . . .

Haunted History

The American Institute of Parapsychology ranks Savannah as the most haunted city in America. It's no wonder since it is a city literally built upon its dead. The great fire of 1820 claimed many lives. Remarkably, that same year, a yellow fever epidemic claimed thousands. With so many deaths, it was overwhelming. Bodies were disposed of in some unusual ways, and mass graves were dug all over the place.

Sadly, grave markers were removed from the slave burial grounds when city expansions were being done, but the bodies remained. Most of the prominent graves, those belonging to African ministers, were moved to Laurel Grove Cemetery. But most of the dead did not get moved to the new cemetery just north of Savannah. Additionally, it was legal to bury slaves in the backyard up until 1818. Over time, the simple gravestones the families posted were often lost as development took place.

For example, when the boutique hotel, The Mansion on Forsyth Park, was built in 2006, roughly a hundred skeletal remains were uncovered during construction. Forensic analysis revealed that these were yellow fever victims. Guess what they did with their newfound discovery? They returned the bones to the site

and continued with construction. No wonder this place is reportedly haunted!

Other lingering spirits can probably be traced back to the early years when men were shanghaied into servitude by unscrupulous and desperate sea captains. Add to that the many men and women who were hanged in Wright Square. One of the most famous to be hanged in these public gallows was Alice Riley. She was the first woman in the state to be executed. She was the servant of a cruel man, William Wise, who mistreated her in many ways. One night, unable to stand it any longer, she and some other servants killed him. They were soon caught and convicted. She pleaded with authorities to spare her since she was pregnant by William Wise. When a doctor confirmed this, she was allowed to live long enough to have the baby. As soon as it was born, the baby was yanked away from its mother. Soon afterwards, she was hanged. A woman in shabby clothing has been seen in Wright Square, supposedly the spirit of this woman looking for the child that was taken from her.

It is also believed that some ancient Indian burial grounds may have been disturbed when the town was founded. The second bloodiest battle of the Revolutionary War was fought near what is now Martin Luther King Jr. Blvd.

Digging up the dead, building on top of the dead, many children dying from an epidemic, men and women who suffered unspeakable tragedies, and mass, unmarked graves make it easy to see why the city is haunted by spirits who have been unable to find peace.

About Savannah

The thing that visitors notice first about this city is the outstanding eighteenth- and nineteenth-century architecture, including the Telfair Academy of Arts and Sciences (one of the first public museums in the South), Georgia Railway Roundhouse Complex (oldest antebellum rail facility still in existence in America), Temple Mickve Israel (third oldest synagogue in the country), and First African Baptist Church (one of the oldest African American Baptist congregations in the U.S.).

If time permits, you may want to venture over to Tybee Island and see some of its sights, including the lighthouse complex and Fort Pulaski National Monument. It is less than a thirty-minute drive and includes some haunted places discussed in the latter part of this book.

Ghost tours can be achieved in many ways, including ghost walks or bus/trolley/hearse rides around the historic district and cemetery tours. Bonaventure Cemetery, just outside Savannah's historic district, is best known for its role in the famous book and movie *Midnight in the Garden of Good and Evil*. It is one of the most photographed cemeteries in America. Colonial Park Cemetery is in the middle of the historic district. It is a popular stop on many ghost tours. Reportedly, many dueling victims were buried here. Dueling was a common practice to settle disputes in colonial days. A couple stories in this book pertain to duels. Laurel Grove Cemetery is significant for a couple of reasons. About 1,500 Confederate soldiers were buried in the northern end of this cemetery. Also, it is one of the oldest African American cemeteries still in existence.

Get a map so you can get oriented. When looking for something, be sure to note the street and square where it can be found. You can walk the entire historic district, but be aware that will require a lot of walking. Be sure to have a plan if you want to see certain places. Go to places in the same area at the same time. A Savannah historic district map highlights all the attractions. They are available in the Savannah Visitor Information Center at 301 Martin Luther King Jr. Blvd.or in the Savannah guidebook that is published every year. It is available at the Visitor Information Center and online at www.

savannahvisit.com. Narrated tours that will help familiarize you with the city and offer some good history and trivia depart from the Visitor Information Center.

Special/annual events: There are more than 200 festivals and special events held every year in Savannah. Go to www.savannahvisit.com/events for a complete listing. A few highlights: Santa Train (December), Holidays on Tybee (December), First Friday Oyster Roast, Annual Savannah Reindeer Run (December), Black Heritage Festival (February), Savannah Irish Festival (February), Savannah Lighted Christmas Parade and Christmas on the River (December), Scottish Games Festival (May), After Hours Tours of Bonaventure Cemetery (November), Savannah Seafood Festival (May), Children's Book Festival, Fourth of July on the Waterfront, Seafood and Music Festival (August), Savannah Film Festival (October), Annual Taste of Savannah (January), Savannah Music Festival (March), and St. Patrick's Day Celebrations (March).

Tours: As mentioned in the introduction, there are dozens of ways to explore this city. For a current list of companies, stop in at the Visitor Information Center or order the Savannah Guidebook online (see Visitor Information at the end of this book for more information).

FAST FACTS ABOUT SAVANNAH

- Savannah is the largest city and the county seat of Chatham County.

- It is the third largest metropolitan area and fourth largest city in Georgia.

- Savannah was founded in 1733 and became the colonial capital of the Province of Georgia and later the first state capital of Georgia.

- Lots of young adults can be found in Savannah because of its four colleges and universities: Armstrong Atlantic State University, Savannah State University, South University, and Savannah College of Art and Design (SCAD). Additionally, these schools have satellite campuses and programs in Savannah: Georgia Tech Savannah, Georgia Southern University, Savannah Technical College, Ralston College, Skidaway Institute of Oceanography. Mercer University now offers a doctor of medicine program at Memorial University Medical Center.

- Millions of visitors come to the city every year to enjoy its expansive historic district, to sample its legendary Lowcountry cuisine, and to explore all its haunted sites.

- You'll notice lots of folks walking the streets at night carrying red plastic cups. Every bar offers patrons "to go" cups in the shade of University of Georgia red. Should you be tempted to take a "traveler" (as locals call "to go" drinks), feel free to do so. It is legal—and encouraged—to take a cocktail for the road!

Ghost Tales

MERCER HOUSE

"Come on, Danny boy. You're acting foolish. Put the gun down, you know you're not going to shoot me," Jim Williams said as he poured himself a brandy. He didn't seem threatened by the young man waving a pistol in his face.

Perhaps he wasn't worried because it wasn't the first time that Danny had pulled out a gun when he didn't get what he wanted. It didn't take much to ignite the young man's trigger temper. And judging by the smell of his breath and slurred speech, he'd already been drinking heavily.

"I want what you owe me! If you don't pay up, I may be forced to let your neighbors know what really goes on inside this house," Danny said angrily.

"I've already paid you this week. Just three days ago, to be precise. Maybe if you didn't spend every dime on drugs and booze, you wouldn't always be so desperate for money," Williams said

with a sneer. He stood with his back to the young man, sipping his drink while waiting for the inevitable argument.

A shot rang out and a vase that sat on the table not five feet from Williams shattered. Williams spun around to see Danny's hand shaking and the pistol still aimed at him.

"You blasted fool! You could have killed me— and you destroyed a very expensive porcelain vase imported from China. I have a good mind to cut you off until you learn your manners and remember where you'd be if I didn't choose to be your benefactor. Now give me the gun before you destroy anything else," Williams said, as he lunged for the gun. But Danny had a firm grasp on the firearm. The two men struggled. Another shot rang out. Danny staggered for a second or two and then keeled over onto the floor with a loud thud.

Many believe that an argument such as this one was what led up to the fatal shooting of Danny Hansford. But was Jim Williams fumbling for the gun when it accidentally went off or was it premeditated murder? Whatever really happened that night we'll never know for sure because both men are dead. The events of this night led to John Berendt's writing the bestseller, *Midnight in the Garden of Good and Evil.* It is a story loosely based on the life of Jim Williams.

The story begins with Jim Williams buying the Italianate mansion on Monterey Square in 1969. Reportedly, Jackie Kennedy Onassis once visited the home, fell in love with it, and tried to buy it.

Williams spent two years painstakingly restoring the house that had sat empty and neglected for some time prior to his buying it. Some records indicate that Williams restored as many as forty or fifty houses in Savannah and beyond. Although Williams considered himself a preservationist, his occupation was an antiques dealer. He was especially fond of 18th and 19th century English and American furniture, as well as Chinese porcelain. He ran his antique shop out of the carriage house that sat behind the large home.

Although he kept it a secret, fearing it would hurt his business and social standing, he was reportedly gay. He had hired Danny Hansford as his part-time "assistant." But Danny was bad news. He was a hustler, alleged drug dealer, and a gigolo. The young man was good-looking and a lot of fun to be around when he wasn't drunk or stoned, which was infrequent. Jim Williams seemed to take the temper tantrums and drunken tirades in stride. He could usually diffuse the situation rather quickly. But some folks thought that he was getting tired of Hansford showing up drunk and out of control. He had recently interrupted a dinner party, and Jim was mortified by his vile behavior. He was afraid that in a small town like Savannah that folks would soon start analyzing this relationship and put two and two together. He may have been thinking that it had been fun but it was time to end the relationship. The final straw had been Danny showing up waving the gun and issuing ultimatums. Jim was surely tired of the threat of "outing" him whenever the young man needed fast cash.

Jim Williams told the police that Danny Hansford

had shown up with a gun and threatened his life. He claimed he was trying to get the gun away from him when it accidentally went off, killing Danny Hansford. The judge found sufficient evidence for trial and Jim Williams was charged with murder. In July 1982, a jury found him guilty. He appealed and won a new trial. Another jury found him guilty. Again, Williams appealed. Thanks to new evidence, he won the appeal. The new evidence came in the form of new witnesses who swore that Hansford had announced he was going to kill Williams. Some believe that Williams paid these people to come forward, but this was never proven. This third trial ended with a hung jury, which meant a mistrial. So, a fourth trial was held. The venue was moved to Augusta because it was now impossible for Williams to get a fair trial in Savannah. The jury acquitted him after only ninety minutes of deliberation.

Jim Williams loved to entertain and was legendary for his late night parties. He threw a huge, lavish Christmas party every year. Now that he was a free man, he looked forward to getting back to tradition. It was the social event of the season. Jim spent hours on every little detail from cocktail napkins to flower arrangements. He wanted everything to be perfect for his re-entry to society. Everyone agreed it was his best party ever. It was also his last.

Within a couple of weeks of this Christmas party, 59-year-old Jim Williams was found dead. Even the cause of his death was shrouded in mystery, as it was never revealed. Some say it was a heart attack brought on from the stress of the four trials and orchestrating the ultimate Christmas party. Others claim it was pneumonia or complications from another illness.

Ever since then, ghostly parties have been seen and heard by neighbors and tourists on the anniversary of Williams' death and during the holidays. The house is lit up and the sounds of a party are heard when neighbors know that no one is at home. Also, men and women are spotted through the windows wearing formal attire when there is no one at home! Sounds like Jim is still throwing legendary parties. . . .

Status: Open to the public for tours ($)
Address: 429 Bull Street, Monterey Square
Website: www.mercerhouse.com

ABOUT THE MERCER HOUSE

The Mercer House was designed by New York architect John S. Norris for General Hugh W. Mercer, who never actually lived in the house. Construction began in 1860 but was interrupted by the Civil War. Mercer later sold it to John Wilder. General Mercer was the great grandfather of songwriter Johnny Mercer. Mercer wrote more than a thousand songs, including "Come Rain or Come Shine" and "Hooray for Hollywood." He died in L.A. in 1976 but was buried in Savannah's Bonaventure Cemetery. Danny Hansford is buried in Greenwich Cemetery, Savannah. Jim Williams (December 11, 1930 – January 14, 1990) is not buried in Savannah. Jim Williams is survived by a sister, Dr. Dorothy Kingery, who is apparently not afraid of ghosts. She has been living in the Mercer house since 1990. She has written a book about her brother. She is a member of Historic Savannah Foundation and turned the Mercer House into a museum that is open to the public.

Note: This is one of the most notable attractions in Savannah because of the *Midnight in the Garden of Good and Evil* connection. Also, it was closed to the public for many years, so be sure to take advantage of its current open-to-the-public status if you plan to visit Savannah.

SHRIMP FACTORY

"What took you so long? I sent you upstairs to grab a bottle of bourbon nearly a half hour ago," *the bartender complained.*

"Well, I, um, ran into a little problem," the employee stammered.

"What kind of a problem?" the bartender demanded.

"There were some broken bottles and liquor all over the floor. I don't know how it happened, maybe they just fell off the shelves. I know this sounds lame, but I didn't break anything. I swear! I don't know what happened, but I knew I had to sweep up the glass and mop the floor," the young man said, wiping sweat off his brow. He was worried the bartender wouldn't believe him, aware of how ridiculous his story sounded. It even crossed his mind that they might make him pay for the liquor. To his relief, the bartender laughed heartily.

"Time to order more rum!" he yelled to the manager. Seeing how upset the waiter was, he assured him that they believed his story. And then he told the waiter that they knew who had made the mess.

"It's our ghost. He gets mad when we run low on rum and he lets us know by trashing the storage room."

"Ghost? Are you kidding me?" the waiter asked incredulously.

*"Seriously. When we close, I'll buy you a
beer and tell you all about it," the bartender
promised.*

Later, he explained the history of the building, which
dates back to 1823. The warehouse was built to store
cotton. In those days, slaves worked all day loading and
unloading cotton bales, the biggest export of the
Lowcountry in those days. At night, the slaves were
reportedly chained or locked upstairs.

Since 1977, the historic warehouse overlooking
the scenic Savannah River became the perfect setting for
a seafood restaurant. The building still has all of its
original bricks, pine rafters, and ballastones (see the River
Street Inn chapter for an explanation of ballastones). The
restaurant soon gained a reputation as being one of the
best restaurants in Savannah. Patrons could choose from
dozens of excellent shrimp entrees.

It soon got a reputation as being one of the most
haunted places in Savannah. Shortly after the grand
opening, unexplainable things began to happen. Voices,
talking softly, were heard coming from the upstairs
storage room. Were these muffled conversations from
slave spirits or something else?

Both the owner, Janie Harris, and her daughter,
Cheryl Harris Powers, think it could be the latter. Cheryl
began working at the restaurant soon after it opened.
Eventually, she took over the business. Like her mother,
she feels it is haunted, but does not know who the
ghost is.

She believes it could be a "newer" ghost—the
spirit of a 55-year-old man named Joe, who dropped dead
one afternoon while climbing the stairs to the storage

room. This was just a few months after the restaurant opened in 1977.

The cause of death was listed as "natural causes," which was strange because the man had no health problems. Some believe that it is likely that a ghost scared him to death.

This is possible given that the staircase leading up to the storage room is one of the most haunted areas of the property. Every employee who has climbed these steps to the storage area has felt freakishly cold when getting to certain spots on the otherwise hot and humid stairwell. Also, when someone goes upstairs to investigate, muffled voices are heard but no one is found. Once upstairs, employees claim to have felt the presence of something supernatural.

In the main part of the restaurant, there are ceiling fans and lights that are controlled by dimmer switches. They turned off and on and moved up and down so often that the owner finally decided to have the electrical wiring replaced. The electrician cited the old wiring as the culprit and assured the owner that replacing it with modern wiring would end all the problems. He laughed when she questioned if it was faulty wiring or their resident ghost. Enough strange things happened during the course of the renovation that the electrical contractor began to believe in ghosts. When the renovation did not help with the problem, everyone grew more convinced that there was supernatural activity.

Is it the ghost of Joe or the slave spirits or both or something else entirely? The only thing known for certain is that the ghost does not like it when the restaurant runs low on rum. He doesn't seem to have a problem with a low supply of whiskey or any other liquor, but gets mad enough to break bottles when the rum inventory gets too low. Broken bottles are never found when there is ample rum in the storage room, so management tries to make sure to keep enough on hand to appease the ghost! The ghost seems to spend most of the time in the storage room, so your chance of an encounter is unlikely—unless you drink the last of his rum. . . .

Status: Open to the public
Address: 313 E. River Street
Website: www.shrimpfactory.com

SEAFOOD FESTIVALS

Can't get enough shrimp? Then mark your calendar for the **Annual Savannah Seafood Festival** on River Street (first weekend of May). There are unique arts and crafts, entertainment, seafood, and more. Festival participants can dine indoors at one of the many River Street eateries or sample all kinds of food offered in tents set up along the waterfront. Also held the first weekend of May is the **Annual Lowcountry Shrimp Festival and Blessing of the Fleet** in the historic village of McClellanville, SC. Besides the blessing of the shrimp trawlers, there's lots of entertainment for the whole family, such as live music, artists and vendors, a special children's area, and lots of shrimp and other good food. Trawlers, fully outfitted with colorful flags and pennants, meander down Jeremy Creek. Following the "blessing" a floral wreath will be laid upon the waters as a memorial to those who have been lost at sea.

OLDE PINK HOUSE

"Did anyone see you?"

"No, I was careful, as always. And my carriage is up the road, not out front. Just like always."

"Good. You know if we get caught, we'll be hanged for treason!

The men nodded in agreement.

The men were well aware of their fate if they got caught. That's why they were meeting secretly late at night in this partially built house. The men were Patriots, also called Rebels and Revolutionaries. Those were the nicknames given to those opposed to British authority. Construction began on the dwelling where they held their revolt meetings in 1771, but was interrupted, like most construction, when the Revolutionary War broke out in 1775. So it seemed a perfect place for their clandestine meetings. The men were never caught and their efforts may have contributed significantly to the outcome of the war.

The house, finally completed in 1789, is a legendary landmark in Savannah. The red brick structure on Reynolds Square was covered with white stucco. Oddly, the red brick "bled" through the stucco, creating a pink exterior. None of the owners liked this effect so it was repeatedly painted white. But the white always turned to pink in time.

Finally, a woman who bought the house in the 1920s decided to paint the house pink. She was planning to turn the property into a tea house. She chose a lovely shade of pink and it has been known as the Olde Pink House ever since that time.

The edifice ultimately became one of the best restaurants in the city. It is believed that the resident ghost is the original owner, Mr. James Habersham Jr. Maybe he didn't like his home being turned into a restaurant or maybe he didn't like it being painted pink. Or maybe he is just trying to protect his beloved home.

James Habersham was a rice planter and Patriot. He held many secret meetings in his half-constructed home, trying to make sure that the British did not win the war. Habersham was a major in the Colonial army. The ghost of the Olde Pink House wears a gray uniform. That is what the Patriots wore, so it is logical that it could be the ghost of James Habersham Jr.

The tavern is the most haunted area. The sound of dice being thrown, voices, and the sound of coins being collected are heard. And the specter in a war uniform has been seen on many occasions.

Some believe it is haunted by more than one ghost. Many believe the second spirit to be the ghost of a war veteran. He has been seen sitting at the bar wearing a uniform. He quickly vanishes if anyone approaches.

A servant girl may the third ghost. She reportedly haunts a second floor. She has been seen and heard crying by patrons and employees.

Status: Open to the public
Address: 23 Abercorn Street, Reynolds Square
Website: www.plantersinnsavannah.com

The Olde Pink House provides room service for the upscale Planters Inn next door.

THE REVOLUTIONARY WAR

The war between the Kingdom of Great Britain and the thirteen colonies in America under British rule began officially on April 19, 1775 (although many people think it didn't begin until July 4, 1776) and ended on September 3, 1783. Significant events leading up to the war included the Stamp Act of 1765 and the Boston Tea Party of 1773.

It ended up being a global war involving several European countries. For instance, France and Spain supplied weapons to the revolutionaries. France openly joined the conflict in 1778. It was fought in America and at sea.

Highlights include Paul Revere's ride, Battle of Bunker Hill, Declaration of Independence signing, Marquis de Lafayette's arrival and participation, Valley Forge, British seizing Savannah and Revolutionaries efforts to recapture it and British leaving Savannah, British capture Charleston and British leaving Charleston, Nathanael Greene appointed commander of the Southern Army, Guilford Courthouse Battle, Articles of Confederation adopted, and Cornwallis surrendering
at Yorktown.

It ended in 1783 with the signing of the Treaty of Paris. The U.S. Constitution was ratified on September 17, 1787.

FUN FACTS

During the Civil War, General Lewis York com-
mandeered the house as a Union headquarters once
Savannah was captured by Union troops during
General Sherman's March to the Sea campaign.

Reportedly, a cache of stolen British gold
was hidden in the house during the War of 1812.

A room in the Olde Pink House has been re-
created to simulate how the dining room would have
appeared when the Habershams lived in the Olde
Pink House.

17HUNDRED90 INN

"I wish you didn't have to leave, my love,"
Anna whispered as she buried her head in the
sailor's broad chest.

"It's my job. Besides, I love the sea," he
replied happily without hesitation.

"Hurry home. I'll be counting the days. Be
safe, my love," she said and then surrendered to
his passionate kiss.

She was so caught up in the moment that she
didn't realize that he never said he loved her or
that he would come back.

Legend has it that the inn has been haunted by a young
woman named Anna or Annie Powers since the 1800s
when she was abandoned by the man she loved. When
her parents died, Anna and her sister decided to use their
inheritance to leave England and start a new life in
America. During the voyage, Annie became close to one
of the crew, a young man named Hans. When they
docked in Savannah, they enjoyed an intense, but brief
romance. When he was called back to duty, he promised
to return for her someday soon.

Supposedly, he knew he was never coming back
for her because he was engaged or married. Some
accounts say that Anna was so broken-hearted and
miserable, that she could not stand the pain. Within weeks

of the sailor's departure, Anna took her life by jumping out an upstairs window, which is now Room 204 of the 17Hundred90 Inn. Perhaps she knew in her heart that her true love had only been having fun with her.

However, the real story is much more sinister. Anna's sister left Savannah to meet relatives. This is what they were both supposed to do, but Anna refused to leave. She argued that the young man would not know where to find her when he came back for her. So she stayed and eventually married the owner of the inn. Annie was only 17 when she married a man old enough to be her grandfather. Not only was he much older, it was a loveless marriage.

Now here is where the story gets confusing. Anna's husband was reportedly a drunk and womanizer— but a wealthy man. Some claim Anna was pushed out the window by his mistress, who wanted to get Anna so that she could become his wife. Others claim that Anna found solace with a young sailor who stayed at the inn. They

fell in love and planned to run away together. Her husband found out and after getting drunk, shoved Anna upstairs. He beat her and then threw her out the window, yelling that "no one would have her now!" No one was ever the wiser until a medium, which was hired just a few years ago, revealed these events.

Whatever the truth is, one thing is for sure. Anna is not a happy spirit. She has been heard crying, and screams have been heard on rare occasions. She steals lingerie from guest rooms and it is later found in weird places. She has assaulted male guests. With a lover who betrayed her and a husband who treated her badly, is it any wonder that she has issues with men?

But Anna may not be the only ghostly guest of the 17Hundred90 Inn. A female cook or chef may haunt the place. A former cook/servant is believed to haunt the property too. It seems she doesn't like people in her kitchen because she has been known to push people and throw things, but only in the kitchen. Some of the employees, such as bartenders, maintenance workers, and managers have had encounters with this ghost. The manager was nearly pushed to the ground by an unseen presence when she was in the kitchen alone one afternoon. The Gullah woman wore colorful clothes and lots of bangle bracelets. When she moved around the kitchen, the bracelets could be heard rattling against one another. The sound of footsteps and pots clanking is also heard, but whenever anyone investigates, they find no one in the kitchen.

The ghost of a little boy may also haunt the inn. He has been seen on occasion running in the hallway near Room 204. Guests have complained of children laughing and running up and down the hallway late at night or early in the morning. But no children were even registered as guests of the property! Legend has it that a little boy fell and hit his head while playing at the inn many years ago. The injury was fatal but perhaps his spirit lives on?

There may be two more ghosts lingering at the inn. The spirits of two maids are believed to haunt it. They like to push their maid cart around the inn and often leave it in the hallway. If it is discovered and returned to the supply room, it is often found again in the hallway. A cart in the hallway is strictly against policy and no employee would dare to violate the policy repeatedly.

Hundreds of guests and employees have reported strange encounters over the years. For example, an employee reports that he was collecting breakfast request cards off the guest room doorknobs late one night when he was picked up—at least five or six inches off the ground—by an unseen force. The experience nearly scared the poor guy to death! As soon as he was able, he ran downstairs and out of the building.

Anna's old bedroom is the most haunted room in the entire place. Many guests who dare to stay in that room have reported feeling a presence. Some say she turns the lights on and off, as she pleases, even in the middle of the night. If a fire has been lit in the room's fireplace, it often goes out for no apparent reason. Former guests and amateur ghost hunters have developed photos they have taken at the inn. Some of the photos show a ghostly shadow. These pictures have been posted on the inn's website.

One interesting thing is her interest in ladies

undergarments. She likes to steal them! A couple of ladies who were not familiar with the legend realized they were missing some undergarments. They complained to the manager that an employee must have entered their room and stolen some of their belongings. The manager was concerned until she found out it was underwear. She explained to the dubious guests that it was probably the resident ghost, Anna. She offered them complimentary refreshments in the lounge while she talked to her staff. The miffed guests acquiesced. On their way to the bar, they discovered their underwear on the lobby Christmas tree!

One thing's for sure. With all this paranormal activity, you are sure to have a memorable experience if you dare to stay at the 17Hundred90 Inn. . . .

Status: Open to the public
Address: 307 East President Street
Website: www.17hundred90.com

THE INN

The inn has fourteen guest rooms, and the dining
room seats 150 patrons. *Gourmet* magazine
has named it "The most elegant restaurant in
Savannah." The inn was originally two houses that
were built in circa 1790, hence the name of the
inn. The significance of 1790 is that it was a time
of change for Savannah. The first elections were
held. This was an important step to becoming a
democratic society.

SORREL WEED HOUSE

"Have you seen my husband?" Matilda asked.

"No, ma'm. I ain't seen the master since dawn's early light," the servant said.

"I have an urgent message for him," Matilda fretted.

"I seen him out by the servants quarters a while ago. I think Molly know where he be," a young slave girl said with a sly smile.

"I'll just go look for him," Matilda replied. She scooted out the kitchen door and down the long walkway to the building that housed the slaves.

The house, completed in 1839–40, has a dark and fascinating history. The mansion is a fine example of Greek Revival and Regency architecture. It is considered to be one of the most important architectural edifices in Savannah. But the Sorrel family only thought of it as home.

It was the first home built on the prestigious Madison Square. Soon after the family moved into the magnificent mansion, it became known as "party central." Francis Sorrel and his wife, Matilda, often hosted elaborate parties that usually lasted until late at night.

The couple had eight children so the house was always full of the sound of laughter and loud conversations. It was a happy home until one day in May 1860 when Matilda caught her husband in bed with one of their servants.

This story begins with Matilda knocking on the door to Molly's room. Without waiting for an answer, she yanked open the door to find out why her servant girl was in her room in the middle of the day instead of at work. What she found was her husband tangled up in the bed sheets with their youngest, prettiest slave girl. Horrified, Matilda screamed a loud, wretched wail as she ran from the room. Francis hurriedly threw on his clothes so that he could catch up with his wife. No telling how he planned to explain this "encounter" because he never got the chance. Matilda raced to the master bedroom where she swung open the balcony door. Without hesitation, she flung herself over the balcony, plummeting to her death.

Her husband was just in time to see her fall. Frantically, he ran towards his wife's crumpled body. But he was too late. When he looked into his wife's lifeless eyes, it was too much for him. He wept as he cradled her in his arms.

Francis Sorrel regretted the affair more than words could say. He blamed himself for his wife's death. He was racked with guilt and shame. Perhaps the servant girl was too. She was found dead just ten days later. Some speculated that he murdered her because he couldn't stand to be reminded of what he had done. Or perhaps she hanged herself because she couldn't live with what she had done.

Francis Sorrel now had two deaths on his hands. He never spoke of what had happened. Nor did he ever remarry. There were no more grand parties. Francis quietly raised his children and went to work.

It is believed that the servant, Molly, and the wife, Matilda, both haunt the property. Residents have been awakened by weird sounds at night. Music and laughter and muffled voices are heard. Objects are often disturbed, moved from their original location to where the ghosts think they belong. There is a huge, old cracked mirror in the hall and a blurry face is sometimes seen in it.

Photographs taken by amateur ghost hunters show orbs and ghostly handprints on the walls. In 2005, TAPS and SyFy Channel's Ghost Hunters conducted an investigation. It is rare for them to definitely declare a place "haunted," but they did make the declaration for the Sorrel-Weed House. The team announced that they had no doubt the place was haunted. They even had an EVP recording of a woman screaming, "Get out. Help me. My God."

For those interested in finding out for themselves, there are a couple of options. There is a historic tour and a ghost tour that includes use of EMF detectors and access to the most haunted areas of the property.

Status: Open to the public for day tours ($). There is information on their website about nightly ghost tours that include admission to the house, including the basement, carriage house, and voodoo room.
Address: 6 W. Harris Street, Madison Square
Website: www.sorrelweedhouse.com

ABOUT THE HOUSE

This house was in a scene in the movie *Forrest Gump* starring Tom Hanks. The property is a designated state landmark. It is one of the most important architectural buildings in Savannah. It was designed by noted architect Charles Clusky. Many important people have been entertained here, including General Robert E. Lee (both before and during the Civil War). It was sold to Henry Davis Weed, a prominent businessman. The Society for the Preservation of Savannah Landmarks (now known as the Historic Savannah Foundation) held their first meeting in this house in 1939.

THE MARSHALL HOUSE

"No, sir. We can't do no more work till CSI
says so," the foreman explained. He shook his
head emphatically to emphasize "no." He had
patiently explained in as many ways as he knew
how to the new owner why no work was being
done. The man had been more than a little upset
when he stopped by to check the progress, only to
find that no one was working.

"CSI? What are you talking about?"

"Crime Scene Investigation. As I said, once
those remains were found, we had no choice
but to call to report it and to stop working
immediately."

The new owner groaned with frustration. It
had taken months since he bought the property
in early 1998 to get to this point. Now he was
being told that the $12 million renovations could
not continue until the authorities completed a
thorough investigation. How long would that take
before the renovations, that had barely begun,
could resume?

But the renovations were necessary given the age and
condition of the property. The Marshall House is the
oldest hotel still in existence in Savannah. It was built in
1851. Mary Marshall, married to Colonel James Marshall,

inherited the property, as well as several other real estate holdings when her father, Gabriel Leaver, died. Leaver, realizing that Savannah was going to grow and prosper, built a four-story hotel. An extensive, spectacular iron veranda was later added. Mary owned the hotel until she died in 1877. According to her will, Mr. William Coolidge was to run the hotel after her death. Records show that Mr. Coolidge raised the first secession flag in Georgia.

A decade later, the Civil War broke out. During that time, it was commandeered and used as a Union hospital, under orders from General Sherman, until the end of the war. After three long hard years at war, there were many injuries and fatalities. The winter of 1864 was fierce. It was so cold and the ground was so hard that it was impossible to dig graves, so the doctors buried body parts under the floorboards.

The hotel closed in 1895, but reopened four years later. When it reopened, the hotel had electric lights and hot and cold water for the guests. In 1933, Herbert W. Gilbert leased the property and changed the name to Gilbert Hotel. Eight years later, Gilbert sold his hotel, as well as some other properties he owned. By 1946, the Marshall House reopened with another renovation. The building has had several owners and sat vacant for prolonged periods of time. In 1956, there was a business on the first floor but the rest of the building was still empty. By the following year, the hotel was closed once again. This time it was due to not being up to safety code requirements. It wasn't long after the extensive renovations began that construction workers discovered remains of human body parts. Work was shut down and the area became a crime scene.

Eventually, they found out that there had been no foul play. Research revealed that the downstairs had been the surgery ward during the war. Once the investigators found out that doctors had put the amputated arms and legs under the floorboards, they ended their investigation and work resumed on the historic property. When work was completed, the Georgia Trust for Historic Preservation named it a National Historic Building in April 2000. Despite the deterioration, the original wood floors, fireplaces, and staircases were salvaged and restored. There are artifacts found during the renovation on display on the second and third floors. A replica of the magnificent wrought iron veranda was achieved and some of the 68 rooms open up to it.

Ever since it reopened, strange things have been reported. Ghosts have been seen in the hallways and entry by guests and employees. Doorknobs rattle late at night in some of the guestrooms, but no one is there when guests go to investigate. A few guests claim to feel something on their wrist during the night, but no one is there. Could it be the spirit of a nurse that was here when this inn was a hospital checking for a pulse? Bathtub faucets have mysteriously turned on. Loud crashes have been heard coming from the fourth floor hall in the wee hours of the morning. The sound of a woman walking in high heel shoes in Room 305 has been heard from guests staying in Room 205. But no guests were registered in that room when these complaints were made! The sound of typing is heard in the room that writer Joel Chandler Harris lived in at one time. A shadowy figure of a woman is seen sometimes near the main floor restrooms. A one-armed Union soldier has been seen walking through the lobby carrying his amputated arm. But the most disturbing encounters are in the basement. Men carrying stretchers with mutilated bodies on them have been seen.

ABOUT THE MARSHALL HOUSE

The author of *Uncle Remus: His Songs and His Sayings*, Joel Chandler Harris, lived in the Marshall House for a while. He found it a great place to write. It has been featured on Travel Channel's Haunted Hotels and named as one of *Coastal Living*'s Top Twenty Places to stay. Guests staying in the 68-room inn will enjoy the benefits of a concierge, free Wi-Fi, business center, complimentary deluxe continental breakfast, wine and cheese served weekday evenings in the library, complimentary bottled water, newspaper, sweet treat delivered at night during turndown service, Bistro 45 restaurant, and guestroom amenities that include antique clawfoot bathtubs, premium mattresses, flatscreen LCD televisions, and balconies on some rooms.

MILESTONES OF THE MARSHALL HOUSE (FROM THEIR WEBSITE)

- 1851—Mary L. Marshall opens The Marshall House on Broughton Street in Savannah's premier shopping district.
- 1857—Ralph Meldrim, proprietor of The Marshall House, erects an iron veranda in front of the property 120 feet in length and 12 feet wide and high. The veranda becomes one of the

signature features of The Marshall House.

- 1859—Having been fully renovated, repainted, and refurbished, the hotel reopens to the public.
- 1864/1865—The hotel is occupied by Union troops led by General William Tecumseh Sherman. The building was used as a Union hospital for wounded soldiers until the end of the Civil War.
- 1867—Marshall Hose Company (Volunteer Fire Department) was founded to protect The Marshall House and other properties in Savannah.
- 1880—The adjoining building, known as the "Florida House," was annexed as part of The Marshall House, increasing the hotel's capacity by about one third.
- 1895—Hotel closes.
- 1899—Hotel reopens as The Marshall House and features electric lights and hot and cold baths on every floor.
- 1933—Herbert W. Gilbert, prominent hotel and real estate man of Jacksonville, leases the building and changes the name to the Gilbert Hotel.
- 1941—Herbert Gilbert sells hotel and eight stores. The property is now steam heated and features a lobby, dining room, living room, reading room, 66 guest rooms, one suite, an apartment and six storage rooms.
- 1946—The Marshall House reopens with a complete renovation.
- 1957—The 106-year-old Marshall House closes.

Extensive alterations to put the hotel in full compliance with state fire laws were not possible on a short-term lease.

- 1998—Renovations to The Marshall House begin once again.
- 1999—The Marshall House, having been fully restored and renovated, reopens to the public as Savannah's oldest hotel.
- 2001—HLC Hotels, Inc., a Savannah-owned and operated hotel management company, purchases The Marshall House.
- 2003—Marshall House featured on The Travel Channel's *Great Hotels*.
- 2004—Marshall House voted "Best of Savannah."
- 2005—Marshall House voted "Best of Savannah" for the second time.
- 2005—Marshall House featured on the Travel Channel's *Haunted Hotels*.
- 2006—Marshall House named as one of Coastal Living's Top 20 Places to Stay.
- 2008—Complete renovation of Marshall House's guest rooms and suites.

Status: Open to the public
Address: 123 E. Broughton Street
Website: www.marshallhouse.com

JULIETTE GORDON LOW HOUSE

(ALSO KNOWN AS THE BIRTHPLACE AND THE WAYNE-GORDON HOUSE)

"I heard piano music this afternoon," the docent said as she entered the office.
"And my computer was on again this morning when I got here. But I distinctly remember turning it off last night before I left."

This wasn't the first time the docent and others had noticed strange goings-on at the old house. Built in 1821, the Regency-style house, believed to have been designed by noted British architect William Jay, has quite a history. It first housed Savannah Mayor James Moore Wayne. He sold it ten years later when he was appointed to the House of Representatives by President Andrew Jackson. It was bought by the Gordon family and was the birthplace of Juliette's father, William Washington Gordon. In 1858, Gordon fell in love with Nellie Kinzie at first sight. They soon married and moved into the home, which they shared with William's mother, Mrs. Sally Gordon Sr.

One of the things William Gordon loved most about his wife was her spirit and personality. Nellie embraced life and never backed down from a challenge—even if it came from her mother-in-law. The domineering woman demanded a lot from her son. Nellie resented her intrusions, most especially that the woman took half of her son's paycheck.

And who could blame poor Nellie? The couple had six children to take care of, including Juliette "Daisy" Gordon. They had three before the Civil War and three more when William Gordon came home after the war. William served in the militia. Nellie used her charm to get General Sherman and General Robert E. Lee to help her find her husband when he was missing on a couple of different occasions during the war. Nellie's charm must have been considerable because General Sherman placed guards at her home to protect her family and brought treats for her children

When the war ended in 1865, William came home. Despite the usual hardships, the couple was deeply in love and lived happily until William's death in 1912. Five years later, Nellie joined William in the afterlife. She died in her bed on February 22, 1917. Shortly afterwards, the

ghost of William Gordon was seen leaving her bedroom by a daughter-in-law. She said he was wearing his Civil War uniform, a gray wool dress uniform. She said he went downstairs and disappeared.

Soon after the frightened woman had her encounter, the butler reported that he had seen Mr. Gordon. His description was the same as the daughter-in-law's, but she had not told him what she had seen. Many believe he came to let Nellie know that they would soon be reunited.

One staff member saw Nellie in the center hall. Others claim to see her staring out her old bedroom window. Another staff member said that the spirit of Nellie was seated at the dining room table when she arrived for work one day.

Besides these sightings, plenty of other unexplainable things have happened over the years. One of Nellie's favorite pastimes was playing her beautiful piano. Music from the parlor piano is often heard, but no one is ever found in the room. Even more disturbing is the fact that the piano hasn't been operational since the 1940s!

Several docents have sworn they have seen the ghost of Nellie's mother-in-law, Sally, all over the house on different occasions.

The adding machine in the office often has a print-out dangling from it with numbers that make no sense and were not there at the end of the previous work day. This happened many times, so the employee unplugged the machine before leaving for the day. Even after the machine was unplugged, a print-out was still found the next day! One time, the same employee witnessed the unplugged machine whirling and computing as if someone were pressing the numerical buttons.

Status: Open to the public for tours ($)
Address: 10 E. Oglethorpe Avenue
Website: www.juliettegordonlowbirthplace.org

THE GIRL SCOUT CONNECTION

During WWII, the house was converted into four apartments to accommodate military workers. It has been the official headquarters of the Girl Scouts of America since 1953. Juliette "Daisy" Gordon Low founded the Girl Scouts of America on March 12, 1912. Her former home is now the National Center of the Girl Scouts. More than 80,000 scouts visit every year. The house has been a National Historic Landmark since 1965.

Strange but true: When Juliette married William Mackay Low on December 21, 1886, a grain of rice punctured her eardrum and resulted in deafness. Due to childhood ear infections, she had already lost most of her hearing in the other ear. But Juliette never let this impediment slow her down. She traveled all over the world and had numerous hobbies and interests. She is buried in Savannah's Laurel Grove Cemetery wearing her Girl Scout uniform. In 2012, the Girl Scouts organization celebrated its 100th anniversary.

ANDREW LOW HOUSE

Located on Lafayette Square, the house was built in 1849 for Andrew Low II. Low immigrated to Savannah from Scotland at the age of sixteen. He worked for his uncle, Andrew Low I, as a cotton merchant. He later became a partner and the president of the Savannah facility. In 1843, he married Sarah Cecil Hunter. By 1848, the couple had three children: a son and two daughters. Andrew Low was a Confederate sympathizer. His attitude once got him arrested as a spy, but he was later released.

While he was building his dream house, his wife, Sarah, his only son, and his uncle died. He inherited a fortune from his uncle, who was like a father to him. Andrew was devastated by the loss of his wife, child, and surrogate father, but he still had two daughters to raise

and a business to run. In late 1849, construction on the house was completed and the Lows moved into it.

A few years later, Andrew met and married Mary Cowper Stiles. The beautiful, sweet young woman was the daughter of an Austrian diplomat, William Henry Stiles. She gave her husband four children: three girls and a son. She was also a gracious host for their many parties, which took place in their two large parlors. They entertained many prominent guests, including General Robert E. Lee.

General Lee often dined and stayed at the Low house when he was at nearby Fort Pulaski. The general had been Jack Mackey's roommate at West Point and the men remained close friends. Jack Mackey was Mary's uncle. In addition to that connection, General Lee had dated Mary's mother before her involvement with William Henry Stiles. Lee became godfather to one of Mary and Andrew's daughter, Jesse.

Their son, William Mackey Low, inherited his father's wealth in 1886. Less than a year later, he married Juliette Gordon (see Juliette Gordon Low House chapter). They lived in England much of the year, but always returned to Savannah for the winter. When both William and Juliette were dead, the house was sold to The National Society of The Colonial Dames of America in the State of Georgia. The group used it as their state headquarters. It became a museum in the 1950s and is open to the public.

The spirit of "Miss Mary" has often been seen. Both Juliette "Daisy" Gordon Low and Miss Mary died in the master bedroom. Many visitors have reported feeling strange or cold in this room. Men in colonial clothing have been seen. A housekeeper smells perfume on the grand staircase and a rocking chair is seen rocking back and forth as if someone were sitting in it rocking. Footsteps have been heard coming from the butler's pantry, but no one is found. These are commonly believed to belong to "Old Tom," a long-time family servant.

Status: Open to the public for tours ($)
Address: 329 Abercorn Street, 912-233-6854
Website: www.andrewlowhouse.com

WATCH OUT FOR CONFUSION WITH THE WAYNE-GORDON HOUSE

The Andrew Low House was the home of Andrew Low (1849–1886) and then the home of Juliette Gordon Low from 1886–1927. It is sometimes confused with the Wayne-Gordon House, more commonly known as "The Birthplace" of Juliette Gordon Low and the Girl Scouts of America National Center.

HAMILTON-TURNER INN

The history of this imposing edifice is absolutely
fascinating. The house was built in 1873 by arguably the
richest man in Savannah. Samuel Pugh Hamilton got rich
running blockades during the Civil War. Proud of his
accomplishments, Hamilton wanted a house that reflected
his wealth. The businessman and jeweler wanted the
biggest and best house in Savannah. He chose a baroque
style of architecture and a tin roof, which saved the
dwelling during the Great Fire of 1898. He went with
only the finest Italian marble, Belgian-cut glass
chandeliers, and superior mahogany woodwork for the
interior. The furniture and artwork was imported from
around the world.

In keeping with his need to impress his neighbors,
Hamilton was the first resident of the city to have
electricity. To show off, he put lights everywhere. It was
so bright during the "light up" ceremony, that neighbors
worried there might be a fire or explosion. Hamilton must
not have shared his neighbors' concern because he kept
all the lights on all night every night. But as president of
the Brush Electric Light & Power Company, he probably
didn't have to worry about getting a bill!

While he might not have been worried about the
lights being a fire hazard, he was worried about being
robbed. With all the big windows and the lights ablaze,
Hamilton's prized possessions were in plain view. To
safeguard them, he hired someone to stand guard on the

roof! From this vantage point, the entire property could be seen. The off-duty police officer stood sentry night after night, armed with a rifle. The plan worked well until the guard was found dead one morning. He had been shot while on duty, and if the bullet didn't kill him, then the fall to the ground finished the job.

A few townsfolk joked that it may have been the next-door neighbor. The man owned the gas company and was not too keen on Hamilton's flaunting the new technology—electricity. Or, he may have simply gotten fed up with the lights shining into his home night after night.

The murder of Hamilton's guard remains an unsolved mystery. Sam Hamilton could find no man

willing to take over the job, no matter how much he offered to pay. So, Hamilton himself stood sentry for several nights before abandoning the idea. His health was not good enough to endure such a hardship. In fact, he died a few months later.

The property has had several owners since that time. One was Dr. Francis Turner, who bought it from the Hamilton estate in 1915. He and his family lived there until 1926 and then it became a rooming house. It was briefly home to Marine Hospital nurses. In the 1940s, the Turners moved back to the house and the basement was converted into office space for Dr. Turner's practice.

The property was sold once again in 1965 to the Cathedral of St. John the Baptist. It was bought for the property to be used as a playground. Historic Savannah Foundation stepped in and saved the house from demolition.

Once again, the mansion was used as a rooming house. The owner was a pseudo-famous person. She was Nancy Hillis, upon whom the character "Mandy" was based in the well-known novel and movie, *Midnight in the Garden of Good and Evil*, which was centered on Savannah and its colorful characters.

Hillis rented out rooms to help pay for maintenance on the enormous house. Tenants reported seeing a man at the top of the stairs. Whenever anyone approached, the figure disappeared. The descriptions always matched how Samuel Hamilton looked and dressed.

Nancy Hillis often heard footsteps upstairs. The first time she was sure that it was an intruder and called the police. They came, investigated, and found no one.

Yet it was impossible for anyone to have exited without detection. Anyone *human*, that is.

At that time, wealthy families built playrooms and bedrooms on the top floor of the house. This was done to keep children out of the way, especially when there were parties. But children like parties and attention. To get attention, the Hamilton children sometimes made loud noises or dropped toys down the steps.

Sam Hamilton had built a big playroom and stocked it with games, including a billiards table. Sometimes, during parties, a couple of the younger children dared to roll a billiard ball down the stairs. The ball made a lot of noise as it clanked and bounced down the numerous steps.

On rare occasions, a billiard ball still appears at the bottom of the stairs. Giggling is heard as the ball makes its way downstairs, but no one is ever found upstairs. Is the spirit of Sam Hamilton still in the Hamilton-Turner Inn watching out for his mischievous children?

A shadowy figure has been spotted on the roof at night. Is this the spirit of Hamilton or the murdered guard? A ghost wearing a Victorian suit has been seen on occasion sitting in a chair at the top of the stairs. This is believed to be Sam Hamilton.

The property was turned into a lovely inn in 1997. It was sold a couple of times and the new owners are Gay and Jim Dunlop. One innkeeper claims she saw a shadowy figure on the roof one night. She happened to look up as she was getting into her car only to see a shape on the roof. The figure disappeared a few seconds later. Could it be the ghost of the guard?

Status: Open to the public
Address: 330 Abercorn Street (next to the Andrew Low House on the southeast side of Lafayette Square)
Website: www.hamilton-turnerinn.com

AWARDS AND GREAT BREAKFASTS

The Hamilton-Turner Inn has won some prestigious awards, including Fodor's Gold Award for Best Sense of Place, TripAdvisor's Top Ten Romantic Locations, AAA Four Diamond Award, and B&B award winner. If you visit their website, you'll find photos of all their lovely rooms and suites, as well as their outstanding breakfast options (such as eggs Benedict and large homemade gourmet muffins).

MOON RIVER
BREWING COMPANY

The Moon River Brewing Company was formerly the first hotel in Savannah. The City Hotel was built in 1821 by Elazer Early of Charleston. When it opened in 1826, the hotel also served as a bank, bar, and post office. Imagine being able to make a deposit, spend the night, eat a hot meal, mail a letter, and have a drink all in the same place!

In 1851, Peter Wiltberger bought the hotel. During the 1850s, he put two lions on exhibit in the lobby. What a marketing ploy! The beautiful creatures drew lots of attention and business—up until 1864 when it was forced to shut down. That's when General Sherman conducted

his "March to the Sea" military campaign. Sherman and his troops left Atlanta on November 16 and made their way to Savannah where he captured the port city on December 21.

After that, the building was used to store lumber and coal. Later, it was used for storage and office space. The roof was ripped off the building during Hurricane David in 1979. The building was vacant from 1979 until 1995 when renovations began to turn the old hotel into a microbrewery and restaurant called the Moon River Brewing Company, which opened on April 10, 1999. In addition to having a great selection of beer, it is known as the most haunted place in Savannah. Ever since that time, people have had ghostly encounters.

"Upstairs is where the ghost resides," Karen told us as she pointed to the old stairs.

The staff graciously shared their stories and answered all my questions and took us all over the building, except to the top floor where no one is allowed. I was in Savannah to research this book and spent one whole evening at Moon River Brewing Company enjoying good food and drink, as well as researching one of the most haunted places in the city.

The story begins in 1832. James Jones Stark was drinking heavily in the hotel's bar. He was what was known as a rabble-rouser. He was a heavy drinker and frequent gambler, so he often ended up in brawls. The nasty drunk began making disparaging remarks about another patron, Dr. Phillip Minis, during a game of coins. When Minis won the game, Stark did not take it well. He accused Minis of cheating and began to yell and curse at him.

Stark challenged Minis to a duel. He chose rifles at paces at 5 P.M. at the river. Minis said the duel had to be pistols at paces at a different time and location. The duel never happened because they two men couldn't agree on terms. The next time they ran into each other, the men got into a fight. They threw a few punches, but it was quickly broken up. Stark continued to malign Minis. Minis grew fearful that the bad talk was hurting his reputation.

On August 9, 1832 things came to a head. Minis confronted Stark at the City Hotel. He was angry and fed up with the things Stark had said about him. He sent someone upstairs to Stark's room to get him. When Stark came downstairs, Minis called him a "coward" and a "liar." Stark, furious at Minis for these comments, lunged for the man. Minis fatally shot Stark. Minis was acquitted at trial. The jury believed what he did was justified because he was in fear for his life. Also, he had his reputation to protect. As Samuel Johnson said, *"A man may shoot the man who invades his character, as he may shoot him who attempts to break into his house."*

The logic was simple: a man's honor was everything, so his reputation had to be safeguarded at all costs. When this was called into question, a duel was often the best way to resolve the situation. Duels could be fought using different weapons, such as swords, pistols, rifles, or knives. Since duels were intended to restore honor, death was not necessary. Only twenty percent of duels ended in death. Andrew Jackson survived fourteen duels!

James Jones Stark has haunted the property ever since his murder. A shadowy figure has been seen. The sounds of a game of pool being played are heard, but no one is there when someone goes to investigate. The cue ball is seen moving across the table but no one has hit it and there is no breeze or logical reason.

A brewery employee was in the office one night doing paperwork when a bottle flew off the shelf and across the room. He heard footsteps on the stairwell but found no one there. Another employee was sitting at the bar one night with some friends. They watched silverware move around on a table as if someone were rearranging it and then watched it drop to the floor, as if someone threw it down.

An antique desk appeared in a room on the second floor. No one knew how it got there. It disappeared three

These are the stairs leading up to the top floor where no one is permitted.

weeks later. No one claimed responsibility for the appearance or disappearance. Once, an employee was in the basement and was violently slapped four times by the ghost!

It is believed that there is another ghost. The spirit of a prostitute has been seen. Employees have heard their names called by a woman, but no one is there when they turn around to answer. An apparition in white is seen stumbling down the stairs. When it was the City Hotel, there were guest rooms upstairs. The clientele was diversified, ranging from respectable businessmen to "ladies of the night" and the likes of James Jones Stark. The torso of a Union soldier was seen in 2007 by a police officer.

The ghosts do not like renovations. Whenever work is done on the old building, tools turn up missing, moved, or are thrown across a room. When work was being done in the late 1990s to turn the building into a brewery, a construction foreman's wife was pushed down the stairs by an invisible force while she was bringing her husband his lunch.

SyFy Channel's Ghost Hunters came in 2005 to find out if the place was indeed haunted. One of their cameras caught a shadowy figure near the bar. How many ghosts does this building host? A little girl in a light-colored dress has been seen. It is believed to be the spirit of a child who died of yellow fever. For a while, the hotel was converted to a hospital during a yellow fever epidemic. The fourth floor housed the sick children. However, a little boy named Toby has been seen on occasion in the basement.

The most haunted areas are the basement and upstairs. When Travel Channel's *Ghost Adventures*

(top) The basement is another haunted part of the Moon River Brewing Company. (bottom) An employee shows us the second floor as part of our private tour, but will not take us to the top floor where the ghost resides.

investigated, they heard dragging sounds in the basement. When they ran down to see, they found no one. Later, they heard knocking, footsteps, and chains rattling, but found no one. Were slaves or prisoners kept in the basement at one time? There are underground tunnels that have been found throughout Savannah, including the exterior of one at Moon River that appears to have been sealed up many years ago. They caught disembodied laughter on tape and heard a female voice but could not understand what she said. Team member, Nick Groff, was briefly possessed when he staked out the basement.

A local publisher, Christina Piva, suffered a bad encounter. During a book party at the restaurant, she went with a group down into the basement. She did not believe in ghosts and said as much to someone who was sharing a ghost story. She was choked, pushed, and grabbed by her neck by an invisible force.

Which ghost attacked this woman? Which ghost might you encounter during a visit to Moon River Brewing Company? Check out their website to see haunted footage that employees and visitors have captured on film and video.

Status: Open to the public
Address: 21 W. Bay Street
Website: www.moonriverbrewingcompany.com

FAMOUS GUESTS

Many important people stayed at the hotel, including
Revolutionary War hero Marquis de Lafayette,
naturalist James Audubon, Winfield Scott (War
of 1812 hero), and three U.S. Navy commodores.
James Audubon lived at the hotel for six months
while he tried to sell his wildlife books.

HAMPTON-LILLIBRIDGE HOUSE

*"In the name of the Father, Son, and Holy
Spirit, I command all Evil spirits to be gone!"
Bishop Albert Rhett Stewart exclaimed.*

Bishop Stewart performed this exorcism on
December 7, 1963, after Jim Williams had arranged
for a bishop of the Episcopal Diocese to come to his
home. He was desperate and didn't know what else to
do. There was an evil spirit in his house and he
needed to get rid of it. His friends refused to come
over anymore, and it had been too long since he had
had a good night's sleep. The bishop performed both

an exorcism and a traditional blessing upon the home. The ghostly activity stopped for about a week before starting again.

But I'm getting ahead of myself in my excitement to share one of my favorite stories. Let me start by sharing some history. The house was built in 1796 by wealthy planter Hampton Lillibridge. The Cape Cod–style house, including a classic New England widow's walk, may seem out of place among Revival and Colonial architecture–style homes, but the design made perfect sense to Rhode Island native, Hampton Lillibridge.

Remarkably, the dwelling was one of only a few to survive the Great Fire of 1820. After Mr. Lillibridge's death, the house was sold—and sold many more times over the years. It was even a boarding house and tenement for a while. Reportedly, a sailor who was renting one of the rooms took his life by hanging himself in his room. Some think his spirit may haunt the place.

The story really gets interesting after Jim Williams bought the three-story property in 1963. (Note that this is the same Jim Williams made famous by the book and movie, *Midnight in the Garden of Good and Evil.* He owned the Mercer House when the events in that story took place. See the Mercer House chapter.) He also bought the house next door. The houses were on E. Bryan Street but Williams had them moved to E. Julian Street. The antiques dealer had a keen interest in historic things, so he wanted to save and renovate these properties. He had already completed one restoration and was looking forward to tackling more projects. However, during the four-block move, the second house was accidentally destroyed during transit. One of the workmen was killed when the house suddenly fell apart. Maybe his spirit haunts the place?

The construction workers uncovered a burial crypt when they began to put the house onto a foundation. They told Williams that it was full of water but they thought it was empty. Impatient and concerned about further delays, Williams instructed the men to cover the crypt and carry on. Perhaps this poor soul haunts the place?

After that, the workers began hearing muffled voices and footsteps on the second floor. It became a routine break for the men to stop work and listen intently to the commotion. But even the toughest contractors became unnerved when apparitions appeared in the window. There were two: a tall, dark man in black and a gray-haired man wearing gray suit or robe. They appeared and disappeared suddenly.

Whenever anyone ran inside to investigate, no one was ever found inside the home.

The construction workers weren't the only ones to see strange things. Neighbors saw figures in the windows too. They also heard screams and singing sometimes. Lights came on and they saw figures dancing when they knew that Jim Williams was out of town. Williams traveled frequently on buying trips for his antique business.

So what did the owner think about all of this? Jim Williams tried to ignore these reports. He was excited about his new home and moved in as soon as the restoration was done. Strange things continued to happen. Maids came and went, scared off by these weird happenings. Williams didn't know what to do about it. But things came to a head one afternoon when the spirit of the house went too far.

Williams was entertaining one afternoon when the group heard distinctive sounds upstairs. Taking the steps two at a time, one of his guests hurried to check it out. Jim pleaded with the man to stop, afraid of what he might discover. When the man didn't return or respond to their calls, the group went upstairs. Shocked, they found the man sprawled on the floor, face down. They helped the shaking man sit up. When he was finally able to speak, they asked what had happened. He explained that as soon as he got upstairs, he suddenly felt very cold, as if he had been submerged in a cold bath or lake. Then he was attacked by an invisible force. He felt himself being dragged across the room. Fearful for his life, he fought with all his strength and ended up on the floor where he stayed, afraid to move.

Jim Williams could no longer ignore the situation. Some of his friends refused to visit anymore. Worse still, he began having ghostly encounters. The most frightening was one night when a ghostly figure appeared in his bedroom doorway. He even approached the bed but then vanished less than four feet from Williams. Another night, the figure approached but Williams got out of bed and walked towards it. The figure turned and fled down the hall. Williams ran after it. The shadowy figure disappeared into one of the upstairs rooms. Williams tried to follow but found the door locked! From this point on, he kept a gun beside the bed. It may have made him feel better, but it wouldn't have done much to stop a ghost!

On December 7, 1963, Jim Williams arranged for Bishop Rhett Stewart to come to his home. The bishop performed both an exorcism and a traditional blessing upon the home. An exorcism is the "religious practice of evicting demons or other spiritual entities from a person or place. Exorcisms were rare until the 1900s, especially the early 1960s through the mid-1970s. As noted above, after the exorcism, the ghostly activity stopped for about a week before starting again.

A maid complained that she had felt an unseen presence and heard what sounded like a chain rattling. Neighbors continued to report activity when Williams was out of town. On most occasions, they said it sounded like a party was going on inside the house. The property was investigated by the Paranormal Center at Duke University. The team concluded the house was definitely haunted. So did famous ghost investigator Hans Holzer.

A psychic, Dr. William Roll of the American Psychical Research Foundation, was also hired to help. After spending a few nights there, he declared the house to be "the most psychically possessed property in the nation."

Unable to take any more, Jim Williams moved out in May 1964. There have been several owners since then. All report unusual happenings but nothing violent or overly frightening. The main complaints have been the sounds of furniture being moved or footsteps or the feeling of not being alone. Once, a door that the owner was certain he locked when he went to bed was found open the next morning. Perhaps that is why indigo blue paint can be spotted under the front porch and a few other subtle places. Reportedly, this keeps the "haints" away!

Status: Not open to the public
Address: 507 E. Julian Street

MIDNIGHT IN THE GARDEN OF GOOD AND EVIL

Midnight in the Garden of Good and Evil, featuring Jim Williams, was written by John Berendt. The book put Savannah on the map and still plays an important role today. It was published in 1994 and remained on the bestseller list for 216 weeks. I think that is a record that remains unsurpassed after all these years. The novel was made into a popular movie. The success is due partly to the eclectic characters, such as Lady Chablis and the Hoodoo priestess, Miranda. My favorite character is the guy who walks the invisible dog! But the characters are icing on the cake. The story is loosely based on incredible real life events that happened in the 1980s. The garden of good and evil refers to Bonaventure Cemetery. The famous Bird Girl statue from the book jacket was relocated from the cemetery to the Telfair Museum in 1997. For more about this story, read the Mercer House tale.

OWENS-THOMAS HOUSE

Construction on this tabby house began in 1816. It was completed three years later. The tabby material, a mixture of sand, lime and oyster shells, was covered with a golden-colored stucco so as to look like stone. An artificial stone known as Coade stone was used too. The architect was William Jay, who was one of the first American-trained architects. It was designed in the Regency style, which comes from England. The young architect went on to design Savannah's Telfair Mansion and many other structures that no longer exist. The fact that 24-year-old William Jay was an in-law of the owner probably helped greatly. Richard Richardson was a wealthy cotton merchant and banker, so he spared no expense on his home. It even had an indoor plumbing system fifteen years before the President of the United States got one installed at the White House!

A massive fire in 1820 destroyed 400 buildings in Savannah. Even more devastating was an outbreak of yellow fever. These two events led to Richardson losing his fortune. The bank foreclosed on his lovely home almost as soon as construction was completed.

For a while the house was an upscale boarding house run by Mary Maxwell. Congressman George Owens bought the property in 1830 for $10,000. In 1825, Marquis de Lafayette stayed in the house for a few days. The marquis delivered a speech from its balcony. It may have been more effective if he had given it in English rather than French! Owens' great-granddaughter, Margaret "Mary" Thomas gave the historic house to the Telfair Museum of Art (called the Academy of Arts & Sciences at that time) in 1951. Her only stipulation was that her former bedroom never be changed. That request has been honored.

Ghostly encounters have been going on for many years. Staff often finds the dining room table and chairs in disarray in the morning when they open up. Everything was in place at the end of the previous day, but they come in to find chairs pushed back from the table and place settings rearranged. Many have complained of feeling an unseen presence.

A man in a riding outfit has been seen upstairs. The shadowy figure of a woman has been seen on occasion.

This is usually when someone is trying to eat or drink inside Mary's former home. This is believed to be the ghost of Mary Telfair, who does not like anyone eating or drinking in the museum house. Once, when staff tried to move Mary's portrait, part of the ceiling collapsed and nearly injured the museum staff. They never tried to move Mary's picture again.

Smoke from a pipe or cigar is sometimes smelled all of a sudden on the porch, yet no one is smoking. The carriage house was once slave quarters. Footsteps and muffled voices are sometimes heard.

When the museum has parties, they are always held outside because of Mary's rules. Whenever they tried to have a party inside, guests were harassed by an unseen presence. If food, beverages, or smoking are involved, the event is held outside. Since this structure is considered one of the finest examples of English Regency architecture in America and contains an impressive

collection of art and furnishings, it is no wonder that Mary is protective of it!

The beautiful gardens that visitors now enjoy have been added. Originally, the garden area was quite small.

Status: Open to the public for tours ($). Three buildings comprise the Telfair Museums: Owens-Thomas House, Jepson Center, and Telfair Academy. There is a café in the Jepson Center. There is a gift shop in the Owens-Thomas House and in the Jepson Center. The museum was the South's first public art museum, which opened in 1886. It boasts a collection of more than 4,500 paintings, sculptures, and other works from all over America and Europe. The Telfair Academy and Owens-Thomas House are both National Historic Landmarks. The Jepson Center offers African American art, Southern art, two galleries for traveling exhibits, a children's gallery, a community gallery, and two outdoor sculpture terraces.
Address: 124 Abercorn Street
Website: www.telfair.org

THE SAVANNAH COLLEGE OF ART AND DESIGN

If you're into art: Savannah is also home to one of the best design schools in the country. The **Savannah College of Art and Design** is a small private college that was founded in 1978. The most popular programs at the school are Graphic Design, Animation, Film/Cinema/Video Studies, Interactive Technology, Photography, Illustration, and Video Graphics and Special Effects. The college is actually comprised of sixty-seven buildings scattered throughout downtown Savannah. There are other SCAD locations, including Atlanta, Georgia; France, and Hong Kong.

KEHOE INN

"Come play with me! Please!" the little boy begged, tugging on her skirt.

She tried to push his hand away, but couldn't find it. When the woman turned around to shoo the boy away, there was no one there! The child had vanished. The lady, who was part of a tour group, became very upset. She interrupted the guide's speech to explain what had happened. Since the Kehoe House is included on many historical and ghost tours, the guide had heard her fair share of strange things. But this was the first time a spirit had spoken to someone in one of her groups.

But the story begins many, many years ago with an Irish immigrant who amassed a small fortune by investing wisely. William Kehoe built the mansion in 1892. He needed a large home as he and his wife, Annie, had ten children, including twins.

The lovely home was a great place to entertain Savannah society with its large rooms, high ceilings, inviting pastel-colored wallpaper, and impressive oak-paneled walls. Annie loved to cut fresh flowers from her garden and put them in decorative vases throughout the house.

Their children, like most children, liked to play

and sometimes did so where they weren't supposed to. The twins died tragically while playing in one of the "off limits" places—a chimney. William had all the fireplaces sealed after their deaths. The coverings are painted with angels, presumably as a gentle reminder of these beloved children.

But are they really gone? The house is now an upscale bed and breakfast. Four-star B&Bs are not conducive to kids, so they are rarely brought to these establishments. Yet evidence of kids is prevalent in the Kehoe House.

Staff and guests have reported many unusual and unexplainable occurrences over the years. Cold spots are often felt, and people have noticed the smell of fresh flowers when none have been put out. The playful sounds of tiny feet running through the house and children giggling have been heard. Yet at the time there are no children registered at the inn—or even seen nearby.

Once, the concierge heard the front bell ring. She glanced up but no one was there, so she did not go to the door. After the third time the bell rang, she watched in amazement as the front door opened. Not only was no one there, but the door had been locked so there's no way it could have blown open!

The most haunted rooms are 201 and 203. Guests have awakened after feeling a touch on their faces. Some guests have awakened to find a female presence sitting on their bed or at the desk. Sometimes, female guests have been awakened by something touching their cheek or hair or hand. When they open their eyes, they see a little boy who soon disappears.

Just like when they were alive, the spirits of children like to play and get into mischief. So, when the doors open mysteriously and lights turn on for no good reason, it is probably just the twins trying to have some fun. . . .

Status: Open to the public
Address: 123 Habersham Street, Columbia Square
Website: www.kehoehouse.com

FOLLOW THE MONEY

When it was built in 1892, the home cost $25,000.
It was sold for $80,000 in 1980. The new owner
was former football legend, Joe Namath. He
planned to turn it into a hip nightclub. The stodgy
neighbors vehemently fought his plans. Just
nine years later, the selling price was $530,000.
The grand house became a B & B in 1992. The
Renaissance Revival mansion is on the National
Register of Historic Places.

RIVER STREET INN

This story is especially intriguing because ghosts are usually heard but not seen. At the River Street Inn, however, there have been many sightings. The 86-room historic inn, built in 1817, spans an entire city block. And the five-story property overlooks the scenic Savannah River—which is no accident.

It was built on the river because it was a cotton warehouse, so boats needed to be able to pull right up to the building for loading. At that time, cotton was the chief export of the Lowcountry, and the Cotton Exchange was

adjacent to this building. The original two floors were
built using ballastones. i.e., material from the ballast on
arriving ships. The ballast was unloaded to make room to
transport the valuable cotton. Rather than waste the
ballast it was used as building material. In 1853, three
floors were added for additional storage space. The cotton
industry was booming. There are all kinds of alleys,
walkways, and bridges so that cotton could be easily
moved. These were also constructed using ballastone.
These walkways have been dubbed the "Factor's Walk,"
because a person who grades the cotton is called a factor.
He must move all through the building to inspect cotton,
so he uses these walkways. At that time, the Lowcountry
had the highest quality or grade cotton in the world.

Amateur ghost hunters, guests, and employees
have seen a couple of different ghosts. One spirit appears
to be a man wearing a suit. Another spirit is a woman
wearing a white dress or gown.

The third floor seems to be most haunted area.

A common complaint is that footsteps and voices are heard when no one is around but the witness. The housekeepers are the ones who most often have these encounters. Doors slam and open mysteriously. A woman crying is sometimes heard.

Status: Open to the public during the day but only to guests at night
Address: 124 E. Bay Street
Website: www.riverstreetinn.com

PIRATES' HOUSE

"Get me some rum!" the voice roared.

"Who said that?" the waiter asked in a trembling voice.

"Get me some rum!" the deep voice repeated

The waiter spun around but there was no one there. He was alone in the dining room—or so he thought.

But is anyone ever alone at The Pirates' House?

Originally, this restaurant was a house. Later, it became a tavern and much later, a restaurant. Some say it was built in 1753, while others claim it was around 1794. Over time, lots of additions were made to the building. When it became a restaurant, these add-ons became twelve dining rooms.

The main level was a restaurant/bar and the upstairs had rooms for rent when the property was an inn for seamen. Sailors on leave rented rooms upstairs, which was convenient after a late night of drinking. Later, it became a jazz bar. Now, it is used as storage space.

Also there is a basement. This is where the tunnel is located. It runs from the house down to the river. Some say that men who got too drunk in the tavern awoke to find themselves on pirate ships, transported to the ship through the tunnel. When these tunnels were built remains unknown. It may relate to slavery or piracy. The remains of a tunnel can be seen today by patrons of the Pirates' House.

Maybe that is why the spirit of a sailor has been seen on the first floor of the Pirate's House and what appears to be a pirate captain who died in one of the upstairs rooms roams the upstairs and the basement. Employees have heard cursing and laughing upstairs, but no one is ever found when someone investigates the noises. A voice calling out *"Get me more rum!"* has been heard. Dining room chairs are rearranged almost every night and doors open for no reason. Screams have been heard coming from the basement when no one is down there. In 2009, major renovations were made to the property, including the removal of roughly thirty-five percent of the Hideaways (tunnel system).

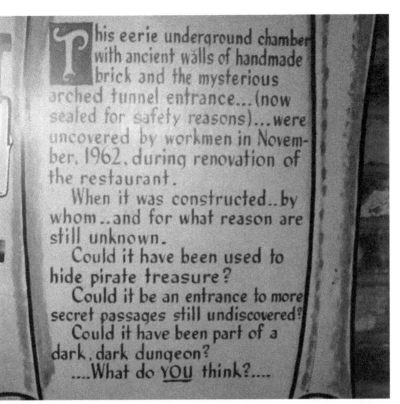

This eerie underground chamber with ancient walls of handmade brick and the mysterious arched tunnel entrance...(now sealed for safety reasons)...were uncovered by workmen in November, 1962, during renovation of the restaurant.

When it was constructed..by whom..and for what reason are still unknown.

Could it have been used to hide pirate treasure?

Could it be an entrance to more secret passages still undiscovered?

Could it have been part of a dark, dark dungeon?

....What do YOU think?....

The Paranormal Ghost Hunters of North Georgia have conducted two investigations. The first was inconclusive, but the second investigation revealed ghostly voices recorded on the EVP.

When visiting, be sure to get seated in the Captain's Room, which is the most haunted area of the building, along with the Herb House. The Captain's

Room is where these seamen once partied, fought, and were shanghaied into servitude. It is believed that the spirits of some of these men still haunt the place.

Our waiter shared a personal experience with us. He explained that one day he came into the Captain's Room

at the start of his shift to check his station. Soon afterwards, table candles blew out and the door began swinging wildly like someone had just come charging through it. He said he suddenly felt a little nauseous and strange.

Status: Open to the public. The upstairs (formerly the sailors' rooms) has been remodeled as a gift shop.
Address: 20 East Broad Street at the intersection of Bay Street (on the outskirts of the historic district, near riverfront)
Website: www.pirateshouse.com

SHANGHAIED INTO PIRACY

Popular stories about Captain Flint haunting this place are most likely untrue. However, men were shanghaied into service by desperate captains. A local Savannah historian, Marmaduke Floyd, says that exhaustive research revealed how the whole thing worked. It was prearranged that an "agent" was paid a fee to help a sea captain or pirate captain capture unwitting men. A hardy-looking young man who was "three sheets to the wind" was the best target. They were lured outside or downstairs where they could be transported to the waiting ship. Many years ago, a police officer claimed he had been drugged and forced into three years of service. He was carried down to the rum cellar and through the tunnel. In 1948, a tunnel was discovered during renovation and filled in. But the remains can still be seen in a corner of the restaurant.

ISAIAH DAVENPORT HOUSE

Built circa 1820, it was a private residence before
becoming a museum. Isaiah Davenport, who hailed from
Rhode Island, built it. Seeing much opportunity in this
bustling port city, Davenport came to Savannah and
began building homes in the early 1800s. He married
Sarah Rosamund Clark and the couple conceived ten
children. His quality workmanship was sought after and
he became wealthy building residences throughout
Savannah.

Isaiah died in 1827. He was only 43 years old when he came down with the deadly yellow fever. He had only lived in this house for seven short years. His widow ran a rooming house for many years after his death. Sarah Davenport sold the property to the Baynard family of South Carolina in 1840.

The dwelling was made into apartments near the turn of the century. They deteriorated into tenement housing. Reportedly, thirteen families lived in the building at one time. It sat vacant for a while. The old house was nearly demolished, but was saved by the Historic Savannah Foundation in 1955.

The architecture of the house is Federal style. It is such a fine example of this type of architecture that the former home was turned into a museum in 1963. Today, it houses nearly 500 pieces of furniture, ceramics, textiles, metals, and more. Roughly 200 fragments found during an archeological dig on site are on display

So who haunts this property? Would you believe a ghost cat! No kidding. It is the only place in Savannah that I know about that is haunted by an animal. The feline has often been seen running around the house and is most often seen by children. You may wonder what is so unusual about a cat roaming around the grounds. Well, nothing, except that the museum staff is adamant that there is no cat (domestic or feral) on the grounds, and cats are not permitted inside the museum. There have also been sightings of a little girl playing. She has been seen inside and outside the house. It is generally believed that she is the spirit of Isaiah Davenport's daughter.

The historical group who oversees the property does not believe it is haunted, despite reports of supernatural encounters from workmen, visitors, volunteers, and former employees.

Status: Open to the public for tours ($)
Address: 324 E. State Street (at the corner of State and Habersham) on Columbia Square
Website: www.davenporthousemuseum.org

HISTORIC SAVANNAH FOUNDATION

In the 1950s, the Historic Savannah Foundation only had seven members. But those women sure knew how to get things done! This handful of women is responsible for saving many historic structures that were slated to be demolished. Savannah has a 2.2-square-mile National Historic Landmark District, the largest in America. There are twelve more National Register districts in Savannah and Chatham County. The Isaiah Davenport House was the first HSF project. Since that time, the HSF has saved more than 350 buildings. It is one of the best local preservation groups in the U.S. They have staff, a board, and an impressive membership of 850 and growing. Their annual budget is around $1 million.

THE OLD CANDLER HOSPITAL

It's no surprise that an old, dilapidated hospital is haunted. Asylums and hospitals are home to much suffering and misery, so, often, the spirits of these poor souls linger long after the place shuts down. This place has a sad, dark history. It was established as Savannah Hospital in 1808 as a facility for the indigent. This is

ironic given that it was later moved to its current location, which is the upscale Forsyth Park neighborhood.

A new hospital was constructed on this site in 1819 and called the Savannah Poor House and Hospital. In 1854, it was converted into the Medical College of Georgia. During the Civil War, it was commandeered by the Confederates until it was seized by General Sherman. It was used by Union soldiers for much of the Civil War. There was a large oak on site. General Sherman built a barricade around this tree to house Confederate prisoners who were wounded.

The facility was also an insane asylum and saw hundreds of deaths during the yellow fever epidemic. Reportedly, nearly 300 people died of fever in a matter of days. So great was the fear of contracting this deadly disease that a morgue and tunnel were built under the hospital. The tunnel was added so that bodies could be disposed of without further risk of contamination. One legend has it that the tunnel was never used for this

reason but for more nefarious purposes. This may be true given that there are tunnels extending all across Savannah. Perhaps they were used by pirates or slaves or soldiers or blockade runners?

The hospital sat vacant for more than twenty years. The Savannah Hospital was bought by the Georgia Hospital Board of the Methodist Church South in 1930. This is when it was renamed Chandler Hospital, in honor of Bishop Warren A. Candler. In 1980, Huntingdon II Ltd. bought the building and it continued to function as a community health care facility until 2000.

Today it is once again vacant. The property has been for sale for a long time. Maybe the ghosts scare off potential buyers? But they don't scare off ghost hunters. There is a ghost tour that includes a visit into the morgue, but that will probably stop soon as the building is pretty badly deteriorated and may pose a danger for visitors.

When the hospital was still open, staff and patients sometimes complained of strange events. The most common was hearing voices when no one was around. Or hearing footsteps when no one was there. On occasion, crying or moaning or screaming was heard.

Status: Not open to the public
Address: 516 Drayton Street

THE CANDLER OAK

There is a huge oak tree behind the hospital that has been designated the Candler Oak. There is a historical marker explaining the significance of the tree, including that General Sherman's troops rested (and possibly camped) under the shade of the tree during their Civil War "March to Sea" military campaign. The tree was in serious jeopardy until it became the first preservation project of the Savannah Tree Foundation. A 6,804-square-foot easement was established in 1984 to protect the tree. A schedule of maintenance was established, including soil tests, mulching, fertilizing, and watering. In 2001, the Candler Oak was designated a Georgia Landmark and Historic Tree by the Georgia Urban Forest Council. In 2004, it was nominated to the National Register of Historic Trees.

FAST FACTS:

Circumference:
16 feet

Height:
50 feet

**Spread
of Crown:**
107 feet

Estimated Age:
280 years

12 W. OGLETHORPE AVENUE

"I've heard that people get physically sick when they go inside the house."

"Yeah, and children coughing like they're sick have been heard, and a woman is sometimes seen in that window," the woman said, pointing up to a second-story window that faced the street.

We were all standing on the porch studying the remains
of this once-magnificent house. Through the dirty,
cracked windows we could see the sad state of the main
level. We did not see a man descending the stairs, but
others have reported catching a glimpse of this spirit.

It is believed to be Dr. Brown. The former owner
also used his home to house his medical practice. Dr.
Brown was happy to trade the brutal English winters for
the Lowcountry humidity. He was quite happy until the
yellow fever epidemic of 1820 struck. He lost dozens of
patients within a few days. The losses were devastating to
the doctor. It took a huge toll emotionally. And he was
worn out from the long hours he put in trying to make his
patients as comfortable as possible.

He was in his office one day when his wife
staggered in carrying their youngest child. "She's burning
up," the woman cried. The father ran across the room and
grabbed his daughter from his wife. Within two days, all
his children and his wife had contracted the deadly
disease.

The doctor did everything he could but he could
not save his family or most of his patients. He got so
despondent that he went to bed and never got up. One
legend has it that he sealed himself inside the house by
bricking up his bedroom door, but there is no proof of
that. Most believe that he came down with fever and
simply got too weak to take care of himself. Having lost
his will to live after losing his family, he probably
stopped eating.

The Elks bought the property in 1908 and made
several renovations. It served as their lodge for many
years. The brick addition on the side was added circa

1970. The building was later used as a Montessori School, and dance classes were given in the ballroom. It sat vacant for a few years before a fire did further damage to the deteriorating property. In April 2009 a fire began in a dumpster behind the house and spread to the house. At one time, the home had pretty hardwood floors, a beautiful ballroom, and a skylight over the sweeping staircase. Thanks to neglect and disaster, the house is a shell of its former state.

When we walked around the house, we noticed that newspapers had been taped over holes, the wallpaper is faded and peeling and smoke-tinged, and the rooms are dirty and filled with debris.

Status: Not open to the public
Address: 12 W. Oglethorpe Avenue

Haunted Cemeteries

BONAVENTURE CEMETERY

Colonel John Mullryne and his wife, Claudia, bought a 600-acre tract of land in 1762. They named their plantation Bonaventure, which means "good fortune." John's youngest daughter, Mary, married Josiah Tattnall. They had two children: John Mullryne Tattnall and Josiah Tattnall Jr. Interestingly, no crops were ever planted at this plantation. But oak trees were planted every fifteen feet along the "roads" of the property.

During the Revolutionary War, Royal Governor James Wright eluded capture by hiding at Bonaventure. French troops arrived in Savannah via the St. Augustine Creek behind the plantation in 1779. French troops used the place as a hospital during the Siege of Savannah. The new government commandeered the property in 1782 and sold at a public auction. It was bought by John Habersham. As a friend of the Tattnall family, he sold it Josiah Tattnall Jr. and his wife, Harriet. They had nine children at Bonaventure from 1786 to 1801. Josiah served as governor of Georgia. Harriet died in 1803 and her husband died the following year. Josiah, Harriet, and four of the children are buried here. The orphaned children were raised by grandparents in London. Josiah Tattnall III, who became a commodore in the Confederate Navy, sold the property to Peter Wiltberger in 1846.

Wiltberger used 70 acres to establish the Evergreen Cemetery Company of Bonaventure, which was designed

around the ruins of the Tattnall house. The first house burned down in 1771 and the second house was destroyed between 1803 and 1817. There's a great story about Josiah and his last night in his house. Josiah loved to entertain and often had a houseful of guests. One night he was throwing one of his lavish parties when the house caught fire. When the servants notified Josiah of the fire, he calmly told them to start taking the food and chairs onto the lawn. Shocked but obedient, the servants began running outside carrying platters of food and a table and chairs. After they had finished relocating the party outside, they quickly turned their efforts to extinguishing the fire. The Tattnalls and their guests, garbed in formal attire, sipped cocktails as they watched the men try to put out the fire. Sadly, fire spread rapidly through the wooden house, rendering their efforts useless. The group assembled on the lawn remained and partied, illuminated by the fire that ultimately consumed Bonaventure Plantation.

Many prominent families transferred the remains of their loved loves from other cemeteries to Evergreen. Peter Wiltberger's wife, Susan, was the first burial that was not transferred from another cemetery. Peter was buried beside his wife in 1853. The city of Savannah bought the cemetery in 1907 and changed the name to Bonaventure Cemetery. More land was purchased and the cemetery expanded. In 2001, Bonaventure Cemetery was placed on the National Register of Historic Places.

A stop at the cemetery is included on most ghost walks and an evening of storytelling in the cemetery is held seasonally because the place is reportedly haunted by several spirits. One is believed to be Josiah Tattnall, who is buried in this cemetery. A figure has been seen wearing formal attire from that era near his gravesite. Also, the sounds of a party (i.e., laughter and music) have been heard on occasion. Perhaps even though the house is long gone, the party continues? A girl has been heard crying who is believed to be the ghost of Gracie Watson. She was a six-year-old who is buried here. Visitors will see her statue at her grave. Some swear that there are ghost dogs that roam the cemetery.

Status: Open to the public
Address: 330 Bonaventure Road

BONAVENTURE'S FAMOUS RESIDENTS

Some famous people buried at the 100-acre
Bonaventure include singer/songwriter Johnny
Mercer; Governor Edward Telfair; Mary Telfair;
Confederate General Hugh W. Mercer; Bishop
Middleton Barnwell, actor James Neill; and poet
Conrad Aiken. The statue made famous in the
movie *Midnight in the Garden of Good and Evil*
(and featured on the cover of the best-selling
book), is known as "Bird Girl" and is no longer in
Bonaventure Cemetery. It was moved to the Telfair
Museum of Art.

COLONIAL PARK CEMETERY

While Bonaventure dates back to the mid-1800s, Colonial
Park Cemetery is even older. It was established in 1750
when it became the only cemetery in the city. Many years
ago, many of the gravestones were removed. One source
says that city officials felt that there were too many
gravestones given that thousands have been buried here
over the years. Their logic was that the markers were
haphazardly placed all over, making it hard to get around
the grounds. And they wanted the area to be a public
park. I have not been able to confirm this, but it doesn't
seem likely that the city would dare to remove
gravestones, but then again, government doesn't always
follow logic! Whatever the reason, there are hundreds or
possibly thousands of unmarked graves so that visitors
are literally walking on top of corpses. A yellow fever
epidemic wiped out ten percent of the city's population in
1820. Due to the many deaths in such a short period of

time, hundreds were buried in mass graves. With mass graves and many graves missing tombstones, visitors are walking over the dead every time they come to Colonial Park.

It was the city's only cemetery from 1750 to 1853. At that time, no more burials were permitted in the overcrowded cemetery. During the Civil War, Union soldiers seized Savannah. They camped in the cemetery during the winter of 1864. They callously vandalized gravestones and robbed mausoleums and tombs—after removing the dead! According to some reports, soldiers removed bodies from numerous crypts so that they could use them as refuge from the cold. Most likely, these bodies were buried in a mass grave rather than returned to their original crypts—if these reports are true.

By the late 1800s, benches and paths had been added throughout the grounds. This was a good start, but hardly enough to placate the poor souls who had been disturbed from their final resting spots or who had been

buried in a mass, unmarked grave. Who are some of the ghosts of Colonial Park Cemetery?

The most famous ghost is Renee Rondolia Asch (or Rene Asche Rondolier, according to some sources). Renee had a lot of strikes against him: he was an orphan, he was disfigured, and he had mental health issues. It was said that he killed animals just to watch them die. And he liked to hang out in the cemetery. So when two young girls were found dead in the cemetery, townsfolk became convinced that Renee killed them. He was lynched in the swamps not far from the cemetery. More murder victims were later found in the cemetery. Everyone was sure that it was the spirit of Renee Rondolia Asch, exacting his revenge. Some even call the cemetery "Renee's Playground."

There was a woman who worked as a maid at the City Hotel. One night, she saw a guest leaving the hotel. She happened to be going in the same direction, so she followed the man down the street. Later, she swore that she saw him literally disappear at the gates of Colonial Park Cemetery.

Footage of a child running through the cemetery has been captured by a visitor. The boy seems to float up into a tree and then out of it and then vanishes. Is it a ghost?

Status: Open to the public as a city park
Address: 201 E. Oglethorpe Avenue (southeast corner of Abercorn Street and Oglethorpe Avenue)

COLONIAL PARK'S
FAMOUS RESIDENTS

Some famous people buried in Colonial Park
Cemetery include James Habersham (Acting
Royal Governor of the Province 1771–1773);
Archibald Bulloch (first president of Georgia);
Samuel Elbert (Revolutionary War soldier and
governor of Georgia); and Lachlan McIntosh (major
general of the Continental Army). Major General
Nathanael Greene was buried here until his remains
were reinterred in Johnson Square in 1901. This
cemetery is much smaller than Bonaventure, only
six acres, but has more than 9,000 graves. The
cemetery closed in 1853 because of overcrowding.
The city developed Laurel Grove and Cathedral
cemeteries. The impressive arch entrance to the
Colonial Park Cemetery was done in 1913 by the
Savannah chapter of the Daughters of the American
Revolution. Archaeologists have discovered nearly
8,700 unmarked graves, in addition to the more than
550 marked graves.

Other Hauntings

Olde Harbour Inn is home to "Hank," who is reportedly the most often encountered ghost, at least in Savannah B&Bs. Hank must like to smoke because guests have complained about cigar smoke, but no one is ever found smoking. Hank may also be a bit mischievous because objects are often moved. No one knows who this ghost is or why he haunts this place. Employees named their ghost "Hank" a long time ago, but that is just a name they chose.

Status: Open to the public
Address: 508 E. Factors Walk
Website: www.oldeharbourinn.com

....

    Eliza Thompson House was the first house built on Jones Street, circa 1847. There are a dozen rooms in the house and another thirteen that surround the garden courtyard. The owners say they have seen the spirit of a Confederate soldier in an upstairs window, and a little girl in a pale nightgown or dress has been seen wandering the halls. If you approach, she disappears!
Status: Open to the public
Address: 5 W. Jones Street
Website: www.elizathompsonhouse.com

Galloway House is a former plantation, built circa 1895, that is now an award-winning B&B. Guest rooms are really apartments that include fully equipped kitchens, private living rooms, and luxurious bathrooms. Guests are given a bottle of wine at check-in and also receive a complimentary continental breakfast. Everyone, including children and pets, is welcome.

Some interesting facts: the outside of the house was painted black at some point and the property has served as low-income housing, a funeral home, a storage facility, an answering service company, and a commune.

The owner swears he was locked in his attic by mischievous spirits as soon as he moved into the property. But don't take his word for it that the old house is haunted; visit their website to find testimonials from former guests who had ghostly encounters.

Status: Open to the public
Address: 107 E. 35 Street
Website: www.thegallowayhouse.com

....

Foley House Inn is actually two mansions, one built in 1868 and the other in 1896. They are now converted into a beautiful B&B on Chippewa Square. When Mr. Foley died, Mrs. Foley began taking in boarders to earn income since her inheritance, for some reason, was frozen for twenty years. Some claim this was the first B&B in Savannah. In the late 1800s, one of the boarders disappeared one night and was never seen or heard from again. The ghost of Foley House is believed to be this mysterious boarder. A male spirit wearing a top hat is sometimes seen at night wandering around the inn's gardens.

Guests will delight in private balconies, whirlpool Jacuzzis, and gas fireplaces in most rooms. The inn also offers a full Southern breakfast, afternoon tea, and wine and hors d'oeuvres in the early evening.

Status: Open to the public
Address: 14 W. Hull Street
Website: www.foleyinn.com

....

Other places in greater Savannah that are rumored to be haunted include: the **Espy House**, **Benjamin Wilson House**, **Royal Tenenbaum's House**, **Dr. Corsen's House**, and the **Savannah Theater**. But I could not find out much information about these places to substantiate these claims. The **Espy House** at 421 Abercorn Street is finally being renovated, but the **Benjamin Wilson House** at 432 Abercorn Street is in sorry shape. The most credible of these is the **Savannah Theater**. Located at 222 Bull Street, it was built in 1818. It has burned down and been rebuilt several times. It is the oldest theater still in operation as a theater and located on its original site. It is believed to be haunted by more than one ghost.

Just Outside Savannah

You won't have to travel too far to visit two more famous haunted sites. And they are worth the trip!

FORT PULASKI

Fort Pulaski is part of a system of forts that the Army Corps of Engineers built in the 1800s. It was reportedly designed by Lt. Robert E. Lee just after he graduated

from West Point in the early 1830s. It was quite the undertaking for the new officer since a large swamp had to be drained so that the elaborate fortress could be erected. He designed underground tunnels and dikes that extend out from the fort. Fort Pulaski was one of 35 forts built at key coastal locations, including Fort Sumter (SC), Fort Macon (NC), Fort Monroe (VA), Fort Adams (RI), and Fort Warren (MA).

It was constructed in 1847 but was not used until the Civil War. The building is hexagonal and is surrounded by a moat with two drawbridges and eight-inch thick walls. The first drawbridge was flanked by two cannons and there was a large cannon at the second drawbridge. There were a total of fifty cannons at Fort Pulaski. U. S. Chief of Engineers, General Totten, once made this statement: "You might as well bombard the Rocky Mountains as Fort Pulaski. No number of guns can reduce this fort in any amount of days."

During the Civil War, 361 Confederate soldiers manned this fort. Supply ships and blockade runners counted on Fort Pulaski. The Union knew they had to

capture this fort if they had any hope of winning the war. They worked at night so that the Confederates wouldn't see their progress. Federal troops landed on Tybee Island and then spent six weeks attacking the fort. They cut off all supply ships and communications. Having many months of supplies and believing the fort to be invincible, the Confederacy was not concerned.

But when the Union began firing new long-range rifle cannons that blasted the fort, the Confederacy soon had to concede the fort. It remained occupied by Union troops until the end of the war. It was a prison for six hundred Confederate officers (called the Immortal Six Hundred) during 1864. These prisoners suffered terribly. They were put on a starvation diet, which was retribution for how Union prisoners were being treated at the time. The diet consisted of cornmeal, pickles, and bread. They became dehydrated and diseases were rampant. Many soldiers died during their confinement. Some were buried in unmarked graves in or around the fort.

With all this suffering and death, it is no wonder that paranormal activity has been recorded. Voices and

moaning have been heard. There are cold spots. And shadowy figures in uniforms have been seen. It is said that most forts are haunted by the spirits of soldiers who died violent deaths at a young age.

Status: Open to the public (free). Gift shop and visitors center on site.

Address: Fort Pulaski National Monument entrance is approximately 15 miles east of Savannah. Take U.S. Highway 80 East. Follow signs for Fort Pulaski, Tybee Island, and beaches.

Website: http://www.nps.gov/fopu

FUN FACTS ABOUT FORT PULASKI

About twenty-five million bricks were used to construct Fort Pulaski. Many of the bricks, known as Savannah Gray, were handmade at the Hermitage Plantation on the Savannah River. Other bricks arrived from Virginia and Maryland.

Signs are posted for visitors to watch for alligators, turtles, and other marine life that now reside in the moat. The marshes that surround the fort are a perfect habitat.

It is amazing to note that in six weeks of heavy attack during the Civil War, all shots sailed over Cockspur Lighthouse. So no damage was done to this little lighthouse that sat in the middle of the battle zone!

One of the earliest baseball games was played at Fort Pulaski.

TYBEE ISLAND LIGHTHOUSE

After Savannah was settled in 1733, it was realized that a lighthouse was needed for this busy port. Less than three years later, a lighthouse and fort were erected on Tybee Island.

The first Tybee Island Lighthouse was built in 1736. The lighthouse you see today is the fourth lighthouse at this location. The others were destroyed by storms, erosion, and war. What was left of the third lighthouse was used as a base for the new beacon. Many changes were made over the years, including the invention of the Fresnel lens and the conversion to electricity in 1933. This is also when the beacon became automated. Once this happened, there was no longer a need for a

keeper and two assistants. When Keeper George Jackson died in 1948, the U.S. Coast Guard took control of the lighthouse. The Tybee Island Historical Society and the City of Tybee Island took responsibility for the lighthouse in 1987, although it still remains under the jurisdiction of the U.S. Coast Guard.

Lighthouse Keeper George Jackson worked right up until his death. He loved this lighthouse and his job so much that he may still be hard at work. An apparition has been seen in a uniform, but it is hard to determine what kind of uniform it is wearing. Lighthouse keepers had to wear uniforms so it could be Jackson. Footsteps have been heard in his old house. The old keeper's house is now used as office space for the historical conservation group. They do not permit ghost investigations and are reluctant to talk about ghosts. But I believe that George Jackson may still be standing watch at his beloved Tybee Lighthouse.

The compound is guarded by two resident cats,

Michael and Miss Kitty (seen above). They are permitted
to roam freely and do, with one exception. They will
not go inside the head keeper's house. It is said to be
the most haunted building in the compound other than
the lighthouse. Back when ghost investigations were
allowed, two different groups spent hours conducting
comprehensive investigations and found paranormal
activity in the lighthouse and keeper's house. It seems
they didn't need to go to all that trouble, all they had to
do was ask Miss Kitty!

Status: Open to the public ($).There is ample parking.
Admission tickets are purchased in the gift shop, which
you have to go through to get into the light station. The
Tybee Lighthouse still has all of its outbuildings, including all three keepers' houses, summer kitchen, and storage shed. They have been restored but maintain their
historical integrity. It is one of the few lighthouse stations

that still has so many original outbuildings. If you feel up to climbing the 178 steep, winding, circular steps, the 360° view from the top is a great reward.

Address: Tybee Island is 18 miles east of Savannah. Going east on Victory Drive, once you exit Thunderbolt, Victory Drive becomes Highway 80 East. Highway 80 East ends on Tybee Island. When you come onto the island, take a left at the first stoplight, which is Campbell Avenue. Follow the lighthouse signs. Campbell Avenue dead ends at Van Horne. Take a left onto Van Horne and the first right onto Meddin Drive.

Website: www.tybeelighthouse.org

Visitor Information

Where should you stay when visiting Savannah? It will cost more to stay in the heart of Savannah rather than midtown or beyond. But having done all options during my visits to Savannah, I recommend staying in the historic district. Traffic can be a hassle and parking is limited, but if you don't stay in the historic district, you will spend a lot of time driving, parking, and feeding meters. It is best to park your car in your hotel parking lot. Some properties include free parking while others add a daily surcharge, so be sure to ask when booking. The cost for lodging varies within the historic district depending on whether the property is a B&B, inn, motel, or boutique hotel. Several of the inns are haunted so if staying in a haunted room appeals to you, read some of the stories in this book before making any reservations. Caveat: Some folks who have stayed on River Street complained that it was noisy most of the night.

It is best to start your visit with a free shuttle ride, the CAT, through the historic district. There are signs posted for designated CAT stops. Look for those or ask at the front desk where you're staying. The shuttle ride will help you to familiarize yourself with the historic district and layout of the city. You can use the free shuttle throughout your visit to get around the city. Be mindful that if you catch the shuttle to go to dinner or some place that is not within easy walking distance of where you're staying, you may have a long walk back as the shuttle does not run late at night.

There is also the option of a narrated "hop on-hop off" tour ($) that departs from the visitor center. This is a popular choice for tourists. (Don't confuse this with the 90-minute narrated trolley tour that is also offered).

As previously stated, there is so much to see and do in Savannah that it can be overwhelming. Decide what's important to you. Did you come to chase ghosts or just see the sights or go shopping or admire the architecture? Would you prefer a walking tour or trolley tour or no tour, perhaps just a quaint carriage ride and independent exploration on foot? Do you prefer a.m. or p.m. activities? If you're interested in touring some of these historic homes and museums, you need to remember that most close at 5 p.m. If you want to dine at some recommended restaurants, be sure to note the hours of operation. Some may be open for lunch only or dinner only or have a limited late night menu after 9 p.m. or 10 p.m.

FYI: All traffic circles throughout the historic district are one-way and the driver in the circle has the right-of-way.

A good starting point is the Savannah Visitor Information Center at Martin Luther King Jr. Blvd. and West Liberty Street. Also, the Savannah History Museum has more than 10,000 artifacts chronicling the city's history. They offer an audiovisual presentation that gives visitors a good overview of Savannah. Additionally, they offer walking tours, self-drive and self-guided tours, free maps, and more.

The convenience of staying in the historic district is worth the higher price to many visitors. However, you can request a visitor guide and it is full of alternative lodging.

Some great sites for visitor information: http://www.visit-historic-savannah.com/historic-district.html and Savannah Convention & Visitors Bureau, www.savannahvisit.com

GETTING THERE

By air: Savannah/Hilton Head International Airport, just off I-16, is about 15–20 minutes from downtown and operates daily flights from several airlines. www.savannahairport.com.

By train: Amtrak stops in Savannah on its Atlantic Coast Service between New York and Miami. The train station is located at 2611 Seaboard Coastline Dr., about 4 miles southwest of downtown. www.amtrak.com

By car: Savannah is just two hours from Charleston, SC (to the north) and Jacksonville, FL (to the south). It is four hours from Atlanta, GA, and from Charlotte, NC. Take I-95 coming from the north or south and watch for Savannah exits. Highway 17 runs through Savannah. Highways 80 and I-16 are other ways to reach Savannah.

Other Titles by Terrance Zepke

Best Ghost Tales of North Carolina and *Best Ghost Tales of South Carolina*. The actors of Carolina's past linger among the living in these thrilling collections of ghost tales. Experience the chilling encounters told by the winners of the North Carolina "Ghost Watch" contest. Use Zepke's tips to conduct your own ghost hunt.

Coastal North Carolina, Second Edition. Terrance Zepke visits the Outer Banks and the upper and lower coasts to bring you the history and heritage of coastal communities, main sites and attractions, sports and outdoor activities, lore and traditions, and even fun ways to test your knowledge of this unique region. Includes more than 50 photos.

Coastal South Carolina. Terrance Zepke shows you historic sites, pieces of history, recreational activities, and traditions of the South Carolina coast. Includes recent and historical photos.

Ghosts and Legends of the Carolina Coasts. This collection of 28 stories ranges from hair-raising tales of horror to fascinating legends from the folklore of North and South Carolina. Learn about the eerie Fire Ship of New Bern and meet the dreaded Boo Hag.

Ghosts of the Carolina Coasts. Taken from real-life occurrences and Carolina Lowcountry lore, these 32 spine-tingling ghost stories take place in prominent historic structures of the region.

Ghosts of the Carolinas for Kids. Be careful in the Carolinas! Do you hear music, whispers, screams, moans, banging, footsteps, tapping, or thumping? Have the lights been turning on and off? Has the door opened and closed by itself? Discover what the Gray Man warns people about and which ghost leaves pennies for the homeowners. Ages 9 and up.

Lighthouses of the Carolinas, Second Edition. Here is the story of each of the 18 lighthouses that aid mariners traveling the coasts of North and South Carolina. Includes visiting information and photos.

Lighthouses of the Carolinas for Kids. A colorful and fun book filled with the history and lore of the lighthouses guarding the Carolina coasts, from Currituck at the top to Haig Point at the bottom. Meet some of the keepers who braved storms and suffered loneliness. Learn how lighthouses operated in the early days and how they work now. Ages 9 and up.

Lowcountry Voodoo: Beginner's Guide to Tales, Spells and Boo Hags. A compilation of some of the beliefs, special spells, and remarkable stories passed down through generations of Gullah families who have made their home in the South Carolina and Georgia Lowcountry.

Pirates of the Carolinas, Second Edition. Thirteen of the most fascinating buccaneers in the history of piracy, including Henry Avery, Blackbeard, Anne Bonny, Captain Kidd, Calico Jack, and Stede Bonnet.

Pirates of the Carolinas for Kids. The Carolinas had more than their share of pirates, including Calico Jack, Billy Lewis, Long Ben Avery, and two women, Anne Bonny and Mary Read. Ages 9 and up.

All of these books are available from Pineapple Press. Visit us at www.pineapplepress.com. For more information on Terrance Zepke's books and future projects, visit her at www.terrancezepke.com.